D0968640

MI 48469

The gripping beast

M WAD   05·01   3713000059227$

Wadley, Margot
Sanilac District Library

SANILAC DISTRICT LIBRARY

The Gripping Beast

The Gripping Beast

MARGOT WADLEY

THOMAS DUNNE BOOKS
ST. MARTIN'S MINOTAUR / NEW YORK

THOMAS DUNNE BOOKS.
An imprint of St. Martin's Press.

THE GRIPPING BEAST. Copyright © 2001 by Margot Wadley.
All rights reserved. Printed in the United States of America.
No part of this book may be used or reproduced in any
manner whatsoever without written permission except in
the case of brief quotations embodied in critical articles or
reviews. For information address St. Martin's Press, 175
Fifth Avenue, New York, N.Y. 10010.

www.minotaurbooks.com

Design and title typography by Lorelle Graffeo

Library of Congress Cataloging-in-Publication Data

Wadley, Margot.
    The gripping beast / Margot Wadley.—1st ed.
        p.   cm.
    ISBN 0-312-27254-5
    1. Americans—Scotland—Fiction.   2. Orkney
(Scotland)—Fiction.   3. Women artists—Fiction.
4. Witchcraft—Fiction.   I. Title.

PS3573.A338 G75 2001
813'.6—dc21

                                    00-047050

First Edition: April 2001

10 9 8 7 6 5 4 3 2 1

MANY THANKS
to those who helped me with this novel~

Kate Green's Split Rock Workshop
Nancy Jo Tubbs
The Blue River Writers, past and present

Judith C. Beale~Carter Elliott
The late Anne M. Faville
Robert Frederick~Sharon Hoffman
Amy Kander~Paul Poff
S. Jewell Ritchey

Beverly Fleming
Jill Bowen
The Fox family, beginning with Anna and Joe
The Yocius family
Ruth Cavin and Julie Sullivan of St. Martin's Press
Richard A. Wadley, my husband

Digerness and its people are imaginary, but
the Orkney Islands, their history, and their many
monuments are wonderfully real. My thanks
go to the people there,
including:

Joann Bowen and Kathlyn B. Kelly, who live
in California~Caroline and Ralph Fotheringhame
and Meg, of Stronsay~Margaret Norquay of
St. Margaret's Hope~Police Constable Derek Robb
and Officer Jim Mollison of the Northern Constabulary,
Area Command Office, Kirkwall

The Gripping Beast

One

Peace! The charm's wound up.
—MACBETH, ACT I, SCENE iii

According to Andrew, there was a witch on board.

He lifted wide, dark eyes to meet mine and said, "Thora. She's here, too, on the *St. Ola.* She's a witch."

His shyness returned and he dropped his gaze. He turned toward the sea again as if still delighting in the view, although the craggy cliffs had disappeared into the distant haze, and this pastoral shoreline could hardly have been less dramatic.

This witch was an old argument, it seemed. Before the boy turned away, I saw the thick veil of his lashes flicker, and saw him cast a challenging glance at his mother, Johanna. Whether she noticed the look or not, she protested only mildly.

"Oh, Andrew," said Johanna, "you know she's not."

"But she is," he said, rounding back to us once more, his shyness already replaced by his eagerness to defend himself. "I saw her."

"Aye, I know she's here," Johanna said patiently, "I saw her myself. She's not a witch, I mean."

"But she told me she was. And once, last summer, I saw—"
He stopped without telling us what he'd seen. He turned to me
with a shrug, conceding to a distinction he seemed to consider
insignificant. "Oh, all right, then, she *says* she's a witch."

Johanna smiled, with a shrug of her own. "Sorry, Isabel. Andrew is right, though, I must admit. The lass does say she's a
witch. But she never does anything witchlike. At least, if she does
I've never seen any evidence of it. Nor has anyone, so far as I
know." She pushed her fingers through her hair, putting on a
thoughtful expression. "Though what a witch is supposed to do
in this day and age..." She trailed off, laughing.

Why couldn't Andrew have seen a ghost, instead? Scotland
abounded in ghosts—romantic figures in floating dress, or wailing,
clanking, clamorous ghosts. They were boasted of or grandly dis-
regarded, or used to tempt tourists into renting haunted castles.
Even the bed-and-breakfast where I had slept last night, that small,
unassuming house in Inverness, claimed its own ghost, though to
me it had remained silent and invisible.

But he'd said a witch, and I knew nothing of those. Except,
of course, for Macbeth's witches. Everyone, even schoolboys, knew
of those three. And Macbeth's witches had appeared to him not
far from where we'd boarded the *St. Ola*, in the far north of Scotland, foretelling Macbeth's grisly future in sweet-sounding riddles,
chanting, *Double, double toil and trouble*...as they stirred into their
pot the eye of newt and toe of frog.

I pictured my schoolchildren in their tattered costumes, dancing around a papier-mâché cauldron fueled by a flickering lightbulb
fire. Without intending to say it aloud, I heard myself only slightly
misquoting a greeting from the play, "How now, you secret, black
and midnight hag."

There was silence for a moment. Then Andrew straightened
and peered up at me, his solemn face splitting into a wide grin.
"Oh no, not a Scottish witch," he said. "A Viking witch."

Two

When shall we three meet again?
—MACBETH, ACT I, SCENE i

I'd met Andrew and Johanna on the *St. Ola* nearly at the end of the crossing.

I could have flown to the Orkney Islands and saved an entire day. Instead of the dawn train from Inverness in a misty rain, then the bus from Thurso to Scrabster, and finally the *St. Ola* to Stromness, I could have boarded a plane in Glasgow as soon as I landed from New York and arrived in Kirkwall yesterday.

But I had come this way, deliberate and unhurried, because I thought my father would have wanted me to. Even now, in my freedom, I did his bidding. And because I sought him as the child he had once been, I wanted to move slowly from my world into that old world of his childhood. Besides, I intended to begin my drawings on the sea.

Almost as soon as the ferry got under way the rain ended, as though reluctant to waste itself on the teeming waters of the Pentland Firth, where the Atlantic stirs itself into the North Sea. Today the seas ran calm, and far ahead the sun streaked down from rents in gray skies.

Above the *St. Ola*, though, the clouds lowered and the sea wind blew cold, and most of the passengers huddled inside, in the lounge or the cafeteria. I stayed alone in the open air leaning against the rail, drawing.

I drew odd shapes and details of the ferry itself, then the seabirds swooping and skimming the waters before us.

As people began to wander onto the deck one or two at a time I drew them, too, rumpled and windblown, all shapes and sizes wrapped alike in waterproof jackets and hats, thick sweaters, and sturdy shoes for a summer's journey on the sea.

Eventually, though, their numbers overwhelmed me, and they came too close for me to sketch them unobserved. I jammed together with them at the rail, all of us watching for the same sight.

A dark broken line appeared on the horizon. The ferry seemed to be barely moving now, stealing closer at an imperceptible pace. The line widened into a knobby wedge. It slowly mounded into a sheer cliff, its red sides plunging straight down into the sea.

I pressed myself against the rail, as if to push us forward more quickly toward the stone column in front of the cliff, its outline slowly emerging from the shadowy background of the headland, becoming a monumental silhouette against the sky.

This was my totem, what my father had called the threshold to the Islands, and suddenly it towered above us, a sea-stack of layered stone sculpted by sea and wind and time into a rough, human-like form.

Now that we were upon it we seemed to be moving too quickly, passing it by too fast. I began to sketch hurriedly, when I heard a voice behind me.

"The Old Man of Hoy!"

The high, light voice was filled with anguish and complaint.

Turning, I saw a boy of about ten, his brows knitted into a dark frown. He held a camera, its brightly woven strap slung around his neck, but he could have photographed nothing but people, nothing but the crowd blocking him from the view.

I decided then I'd seen so many pictures of the Old Man, heard my father describe it so often, read of it so recently in his journal, I didn't need to draw it now. I shoved my sketchbook into my pocket and stepped back, giving the boy my own small space in the crowd. "Come up here, there's plenty of room."

His face brightened. He slid a shy, sidelong smile to me as he squeezed in and began to snap pictures.

"Thank you," said a woman, a not much taller version of the boy, the same round face and dark eyes, and short black hair whose waves blew in tangles around her head. "Andrew has seen this many times, but he's not had a camera before. He's been so looking forward to photographing it."

At that moment the clouds parted above us. The sun's rays lit the red stone of the cliffs with fire, cutting the fissures and black caves deep into its sides. We watched together in silence.

After a few minutes the woman spoke again. "You're an American, aren't you?" Her words rolled out with a soft burr. "Are you on holiday, then?"

"Yes," I said, only partly truthfully, since my holiday was primarily a pilgrimage. "My first visit to the Orkney Islands."

Because of her accent, I added, "And you're Scottish, but not from Orkney. I can tell."

"However did you know?"

"My father was born in Orkney. He left while still a boy so he lost much of his accent, but he could still conjure it up to tease me. I never understood a word he said."

She laughed. "I'm certain he thickened it a wee bit. You'll be used to it in no time, as we are—though we hear it often, every summer, and occasionally at Christmas. We live in Inverness, you see, but each year Andrew and I leave his father at home and spend the school holidays with my aunt and uncle."

She looked wistfully at her son. "I suppose one day he'll not want to travel with his mother, but for now he finds coming here quite wonderful. He likes best being on the farm, though there's much else for you. Ancient places and natural wonders, and beautiful scenery."

I nodded. "To my father there was nowhere like Orkney. He always planned to visit once again, but he didn't, not since almost forty years ago."

I stopped for a minute to allow the unexpected tightness in my throat to ease. "So I've come back in his place, back to Digerness."

Blinking away imminent tears, I stared out at the shore. The island of Hoy and its precipitous coast lay behind us. We passed a few small, bleak islands, and a lighthouse on a rocky point. New land appeared, the coast of Mainland, the largest of the Orkney Islands, with farms nestled among gentle hills and pastures running down to the sea.

"Back to Digerness?" Andrew, joining us, echoed my words. His camera, in this unspectacular landscape, was tucked into the front of his jacket. "That's where we're going, too."

"It seems we'll be neighbors, for a while at least," the woman said, and held out her hand. "I'm Johanna MacLeod, and this is my son, Andrew."

"I'm Isabel Garth."

I glanced around. "Isn't it odd that we should meet?" Most of the other passengers would be tourists, and among them a few historians and photographers. Several would be staying in Stromness, heading to fishing lodges on the lochs, or traveling on to the smaller islands. But most would be going to Kirkwall. "Odd, that of all of the people on board, we three should be going to Digerness?"

"But there's one more," Andrew had said then, dancing a little in his excitement. "One more of us going to Digerness. Thora."

It was then he had turned his eyes to mine, and told me, "Thora. She has the farm next to my Nana and Uncle John. She's here, too, on the *St. Ola.* She's a witch."

The *St. Ola* blew her whistle. We had reached Stromness, and suddenly the crowd became lively. Drivers bustled to go below, to get into their cars. The rest of us funneled down the stairs to our luggage and to the passenger doors.

"Uncle John's collecting us," Johanna said. "Perhaps you'd like to—?"

I shook my head. "Thanks. But I'm told a bus will be waiting, and it will take me right to my hotel."

"You'll be coming to the Festival on Tuesday? A wee summer celebration by the village, just for fun. Except this year we're celebrating even more, because we're not going to have a nuclear-waste site after all." Johanna, holding tight to Andrew's hand, was being borne apart from me by the tide of passengers. "We'll see you there."

"But where?"

"Everywhere. All over town. Come to the craft co-op, we'll most likely be there, with Nan. Her quilts..." They were drifting farther away. "Spindrift," Johanna called, over the crowd. "You'll find it. Ask anyone." She waved. "See you there."

Since today was Thursday, I didn't expect to meet them again for almost a week. But as I reached the end of the pier and rounded the corner toward my waiting bus, I saw them standing beside an aged dark green Volkswagen Beetle.

Johanna and Andrew were talking to a young woman who stood in the half-open driver's door, as though she'd frozen in mid-motion while climbing in or out. Tall and gangling, she looked

barely out of her teens. Her coppery hair, tied into an unfashion-
able bun, fought a losing battle, less against the wind than her
own springy, bristly curls. Like the rest of us she wore jeans and
rain gear, but her hooded coat was orange, almost the color of her
hair. She would have been easy to spot on the *St. Ola.* I hadn't
seen her, but I was sure she'd been there. This had to be Thora,
Andrew's witch.

Andrew confirmed it. Seeing me, he waved, and called me over.

Up close, Thora still looked young. Across her nose and
cheeks lay a light scatter of freckles, like a dappled shadow across
her face. Yet cool, blue eyes gave her a serene, faraway look. Although only slightly taller than I was, she seemed to look down
haughtily at me.

But when she reached out her hand and our fingers touched,
her complexion, already pale against her florid hair, paled further
still. Her freckles stood out in dark relief as a startled expression
crossed her face. I wondered if she was going to faint, but she
simply sucked in her breath and let it out sharply, making a small
sound.

"Oh!"

Without taking another breath, she again made a sound, qui-
eter than the first.

"Go."

She said it so softly I wasn't sure the second word was not
the same as the first. But she repeated it.

"Go," said Andrew's witch. "There is danger here for you. I
can feel it. Go home."

I should have laughed, and Johanna and Andrew with me, but
not one of us did. Not one of us spoke. Johanna, standing behind
Andrew, wrapped her arms protectively around him.

I was dimly aware of people moving past us, of people getting
into cars and driving away to homes and hotels. I could see my

bus waiting at the end of the street, ready to leave, with or without me, as soon as its scheduled departure time arrived.

Still no one spoke. I couldn't move. Thora dove into her car and started it with a jarring grind. She shot off, maneuvering jerkily around small knots of people, past the Harbor Office and the Stromness Hotel, and disappeared into the winding granite streets of the town.

Three

. . . Let's after him,
Whose care is gone before to bid us welcome.
—MACBETH, ACT I, SCENE iv

I don't believe in witches," I said, breaking the silence that hung over us. A gust of wind blew down the narrow stone canyon of the street, and I shivered.

Johanna gave me a questioning look, unwound her arms from around Andrew, and placed a hand on my arm. She'd noticed my shiver but, taking the wind for granted, misinterpreted its cause.

I hastened to reassure her. "I'm not upset. I wasn't frightened, only . . ."

I tried to remember how I'd felt, tried to remember feeling anything except astonishment—not that this girl who claimed to be a witch should say what she had, but that she should have said it to me. With an apologetic glance at Andrew, I said again, "I don't believe in witches. I don't believe in portents, either. And I do not believe in Thora."

"Nor do we!" Johanna exclaimed. Still, she held tight to my arm and said, "But you can't take the bus, now, all by yourself.

Don't argue, Isabel. Uncle John will be here momentarily. You'll come with us in his car."

And the bus, settling the issue on its own, closed its doors and pulled away.

Andrew, freed now from his mother's embrace, spoke for the first time. He alone had seemed unshaken by Thora's behavior. His composed expression suggested it had been no more than he'd expected. She was, after all, a witch. But he, too, touched my arm. "I'm sorry," he said gravely, as if he had been to blame.

Then John Rousay arrived, his tan station wagon threading its careful way down to the end of the street where we waited.

Andrew brightened, plainly glad to see him, but plainly eager, too, to be the one to tell of the afternoon's drama.

"Whoa, lad, let me look at you first." Uncle John's voice rose and fell in the local rhythm, bringing echoes of Scandinavia into its Scot's burr. He held Andrew at arm's length with a large, gentle hand. He took off his hat, a brown knitted tam with a bobble in its center, and held it over his chest while he regarded Andrew seriously. Then, looking at Johanna with pale blue eyes that peered from lined, weathered lids in a way that suggested he'd spent all of his days in wind and glare, he said, "Aye, he's grown a wee bit." He gathered them both into his arms, his face shining.

He listened to Andrew's story, his head cocked to one side, a frown gathering as he took it all in. Then he turned to me with a shake of his head. "We'll see she's spoken to. Nan will know what to say. No matter what, we canna have Thora going round upsetting people in this way." He folded both of my hands in his and said kindly, "Ach, the poor lass."

But I wasn't quite sure if he was referring to me or to Thora.

John drove out of the town in the same slow, careful way he had driven in. I saw him take his eyes from the road only once, to cast a worried glance at Andrew sitting quietly on the seat beside him. I guessed Andrew ought to be chattering away about his trip, about his new camera, or questioning John about the latest happenings at the farm.

Johanna tried to prompt him. "Andrew, tell Uncle John about the birds we saw this morning," but Andrew murmured only a brief response, a mere list. He was brooding, after all, about Thora.

We drove on in an unhappy silence, leaving the town behind. Instead of the savage landscape I might have expected from my first glimpse of the Islands, I saw only fields blowing with buttercups and daisies and Queen Anne's lace. Fences carved low hills into green rectangles. Slabs of stone, supplanting fence posts, listed about here and there like widely scattered grave markers. No trees divided the fields or interrupted the view, which seemed to extend forever.

Beyond low pastures lay a shimmer of flat, bright water and distant dark purple hills, with black clouds trailing over them like smoke.

"Look!" said Andrew into the quiet, and I felt Johanna relax beside me. Andrew had turned and was pointing, directing my gaze toward the water and beyond. "Look, the Stones of Stenness."

On a narrow strip of land, which separated the water into two large lochs, within the fence-stitched patchwork of a farmer's fields, stone monoliths reached to the sky.

"And the Ring of Brodgar. You can see them both from here. Ancient rings, like Stonehenge. Look."

Several angled stones strung themselves along the land between the lochs, and some stood in small groups. I could see them jagging upward, though I could not distinguish which were which, nor make out the rings that Andrew said they formed. I would come back another day, tomorrow perhaps, to see them closer, to walk among them, to touch the stones and look up at their great heights. Because my father, too, had walked among them, and had left me their stories in his journals.

"And the Watch Stone between them," said Andrew, bringing me back. "Can you see it, the tallest one?"

I couldn't, but Andrew continued unabashed. "They say it walks sometimes, down to the loch to have a drink." He grinned. Everyone told this story, this popular myth, but no one pretended to believe it. It was safe.

It was a reminder, though, a mention of magic, and his stillness returned. It wasn't long before he twisted around in his seat and said doubtfully to his mother, "Suppose she is real? Suppose Thora isn't a fake?"

"She isn't a fake, Andrew, not truly. She's just making things up, dramatizing herself. You know she loves to do that, to get attention. She simply went too far this time. And she knew it. You saw how she looked, so pale and frightened. And embarrassed. That's why she ran away from us. She's probably regretting it by now. You'll see her at the Festival, or before, at the farm, and she'll be her old self."

Andrew studied my face as if to see if I accepted his mother's reasoning. He gave a satisfied nod, then settled back to begin a lively conversation with Uncle John.

With Andrew behaving normally, Johanna turned her attention to me, to offer an explanation of Thora. For my comfort, or for Thora's absolution?

"Thora isn't her real name. She was called Theresa—Theresa Stannay. She doesn't use her surname anymore, and she long ago decided Theresa was too common." Johanna's face softened, and she added, "But perhaps I judge her too harshly. For a Scot, Theresa is exotic enough. And Thora is a Viking name, full of drama, to be sure, but Orkadian. True to her heritage."

Johanna paused, and seemed to be reaching into her memories before continuing. "She used to be an ordinary Orkney girl—well, she's always been a little different. Artistic. But not so intense, so determined to be odd. Not until she went away to art school. Not until her parents died."

Any anger I'd felt at having been used in Thora's performance was ebbing away. An odd girl, who never fit in until art school, and now was left alone—not the same as me, exactly, but close enough. Especially now.

"Both her parents? At once?" I asked. At her nod I said, "It must have been in an accident."

"They were drowned."

Andrew turned to us again. He said, matter-of-factly, "In the haar."

"The haar?"

"A summer storm, a sea fog," Johanna said. "Very dense and sudden, on an otherwise fine day, a hot summer day. Thora's parents were experienced sailors, but even so they were caught in it and they never came back. And Thora came home from school, poor lamb, to an empty house and a lonely farm."

"But what did she do?"

"She continued her parents' farming at first. Hers is but a wee holding, and the neighbors helped, didn't you, John?"

"Aye, we tried. But her farming didn't last for long. For a peedie lass by herself the work was too much, and her heart was not in it. She keeps but a few sheep now, special sheep for her special wool."

"She weaves, you see," Johanna said. "Beautiful creations. She sells them at Spindrift and the shops in Kirkwall, but she's becoming quite successful elsewhere. That's why she was on the *St. Ola*, returning from London where she's been selling to one of the large shops. So naturally we were surprised by the way she behaved."

Johanna leaned closer and said with concern, "I hope you won't let it spoil your holiday."

"Of course it won't." I laughed then, as I should have done

at the start. "Her words had nothing to do with me. She was simply being dramatic. You said so yourself. Don't worry. I know I'll have a wonderful time."

I heard a spattering on the windows, and looked up to see them blurred with rain. We must have been climbing slowly for some time, climbing into the cloud-shrouded hills I'd seen earlier.

"Digerness," Andrew announced.

I etched onto my mind each change of scene as we followed the road, as it turned and descended again toward the sea, displaying the village below us. Gray houses wound in rambling rows along the waterfront, their slate roofs gleaming like pewter in the mist.

John, who, except for his few sympathetic words about Thora, had spoken only with Andrew, now said to me with some shyness, "My wife will be unhappy when she learns she missed you. Nan will be wanting to meet you, I ken."

"Isabel's coming to the Festival," Andrew said. "She can meet Nana then.

"She's not my granny, truly," he explained to me, "but I've called her Nana all my life. Because of her name, you see. Besides, she's like a granny to me."

A new idea lit his eyes, and he said, "You can come to Otterness Farm as well." He turned to his mother for approval. "She can, can't she? I can show her," here he paused dramatically and opened his arms wide, "everything."

"She may, Andrew, but I do think you should ask Isabel herself, don't you?"

"Will you come to visit us?" he asked. "I'll show you something special. Promise you will!"

"Come Wednesday," Johanna added. "The day after the Festival, when we've finished with all that work." She waved away my protest. "You'll be ready for a home-cooked meal by then. Come early, so Andrew can show you round. And you can tell us all about your holiday so far. We'll not take no for an answer."

John had stopped the car in front of the inn, a stone building whose dormer windows looked out over the small harbor. Carved into the stone above the door was its name, Furrowend.

"Thank you for befriending me, for bringing me here. I'm glad we happened to meet. I'd love to visit the farm. I'll look forward to your tour, Andrew, but I'll see you first at the Festival."

John wanted to carry my bag into the inn, but that at least I was able to refuse. "Thank you, but I can handle it.

"I'm used to being on my own," I added, as though saying that might make it true. I'd wished it for so long, to please only myself, to care only for myself. But now that I had endured the losses that made it so, I wondered if I truly wanted it. And I was sure, now, I would not be on my own for very long.

I stood in the light rain waving as my new friends drove off, and watched until they drew out of sight.

And I watched a green Volkswagen Beetle creep out of the parking lot beside the inn and drive off in the same direction.

Inside, a red tartan carpet and white walls brightened the small lobby. French doors, closed now, led to a restaurant that must have taken up much of the main floor. Across from the doors, two upholstered chairs sat on either side of a gas-log fireplace. At the back the reception desk stretched between a staircase and a side wall.

A man leaned over the desk. Beyond him, a young woman looked up at him from behind the counter. Their heads close together, they made a handsome pair, his hair black, hers a flaxen halo around her head. At first I thought he was lounging there, flirting with her, until I noticed the rigidity of his back and the anxiety on her face. They were quarreling.

I hung back, unsure if I should interrupt, when the woman saw me.

She leaped up. A reflection of tears glittered in her eyes. "Are you Isabel Garth? Thank goodness you're here. I've been so worried." Reproach sounded in her voice, and she must have heard it herself, for she said, "I'm sorry, I don't mean to scold. Only, you wrote that you'd arrive on the bus, and when it showed up without you, I didn't know what to think. But here you are." She smiled, relieved, and offered her own explanation. "I expect you've had a lift."

When I agreed, she shot a triumphant look at the scowling man and said, "There, you see, she's had a lift," as though their disagreement had been about my probable fate. "Come, I'll show you to your room."

Her lilting voice went ahead of me as I followed her up the stairs. "My name is Meggie Denison. If you need anything, you've only to ask. Or ring the wee bell on the desk if you don't see me. You'll have your breakfast in the restaurant. Dinner as well, if you wish it. We're open to the public for dinner."

The top of the stairs opened to a dormered lounge, with deep chairs, a television, and a fireplace like the one downstairs. Down a short corridor, past a pay-phone in a booth fitted into a corner, Meggie led me into my room.

Flowers were everywhere. They bloomed over the walls and the bedding, and flower-curtained windows looked out over the harbor below. Gesturing to an electric kettle next to a flowered tea set on the dresser, Meggie said, "You'll be wanting tea after your journey, but something to eat as well, I expect. We'll open soon for dinner, so come down whenever you're ready."

I was anxious to begin my exploration, though, to see something, however little, of the village. When I went downstairs I said, "I'd like to go for my car, I think. I have one reserved at Duncan's Garage. Is it far? Is there time before dinner?"

"There's time, of course, but..."

I followed her gaze to the narrow window beside the front door. The mist had become a sheeting rain.

"I'll go in the morning, then, I suppose."

"No need." The man, smiling now, rose from one of the fire-place chairs and sauntered over to join us. "I'll take you there myself right now, shall I?"

Meggie looked at him, a brief flicker of surprise widening her eyes. Then it was gone, and she said, "This is my friend Ross. Ross MacDonald."

She shrugged. "The day may be fair tomorrow, or it may be like this again. Our weather..." She smiled ruefully. "So perhaps, since Ross has offered.... If you'd like, I'll call Davey Duncan and tell him you're coming."

"I'll bring my car around, then." Ross smiled down at me, and was gone.

His car, a black Land Rover, had a high cab requiring a high step into it. Ross held the door open, then helped me in, an arm around my waist and a hand holding mine.

"We don't get many Americans here," he said as we started up one of the stone-flagged streets that climbed from the half-moon of the bay, "though we're close enough to the more popular sights. Too quiet, perhaps. But then, some prefer that."

He negotiated around cars parked in the narrow lane, then took his eyes from the road to study me as he asked, "And what is it you're doing in Digerness?"

"My father was born here. I wanted to visit, to see where he grew up." I added, "He died not long ago."

Ross offered no sympathy, just a nod, either of understanding or simple acknowledgment of the answer to his question. Was that what he'd wanted to learn, why he'd offered, to Meggie's surprise, to drive me?

"You'll be touring, then, tomorrow?" he asked conversationally, his curiosity satisfied. "Meggie will tell you where to go. Part of her job it is, directing tourists, as well as running the inn."

"Alone? A big job for one person."

"Aye, but they've only the four rooms. The inn belongs to her parents, you see. They run the restaurant, and leave the rest for Meggie to manage." His tone turned querulous. "They all live right there as well, so the work goes on full-time, like farming. Their whole life. Someday I'll—"

He broke off. We'd reached Duncan's Garage, and he pulled the Rover into the dry covered forecourt. "I'll let you out here, shall I?"

He didn't help me out as he had helped me in. Instead, he reached across to open my door. He leaned close, and I was aware of his blue eyes, his face inches from mine, of his breath warm on my cheek, of his arm almost embracing me. The instant the door opened I slid out, my feet landing heavily on the ground.

Ross called after me, "Enjoy your holiday. I'm sure you will. Orkney is full of surprises." Then he took off into the rain.

I drove the short distance back to the inn slowly, concentrating on keeping my bright red Renault on my own side of the road.

Although at the garage an assured young man with *Davey* embroidered on his coverall pocket had explained, with exaggerated patience, the workings of the car and the vagaries of foreign driving, I'd expected to have no difficulty. But right away, pulling out from the garage, I'd turned into the wrong side of the road. I should have waited until morning for this, I scolded myself, until the rain had stopped and I'd had a good night's sleep. I quickly corrected, but when my eyes finally found the rearview mirror I saw Davey Duncan and two other men watching, wide grins lighting their faces, and I ran the car up over the left-hand curb.

The rain ended before I finished dinner. From my table I watched the clouds blow away, leaving the sky as bright as midday. Families strolled the waterfront, and the high voices of the children floated in through the windows. Boats bobbed at their moorings, their nets, brilliant with orange floats, ready on their decks. I knew it would stay light for hours more, until midnight almost. A walk tempted me, but not as much as my bed, beneath its flowered quilt.

I went upstairs, but not yet to sleep. I needed to do one more thing before bed.

For a few minutes I worried that I'd lost the letters I was sure I'd folded among my blouses in my carryall. Ben Gowan, my father's childhood friend, was, like Uncle John, a Digerness farmer, though he had stayed and my father had left. They corresponded for more than forty years. I'd read only a few of the most recent letters, and never really understood how the two could find so much to discuss after so many years, but when my father's illness reached its final stage Ben Gowan wrote to me a kind, sensible letter of hope and encouragement. And later, after I'd informed him of my father's death, after he'd sent his condolences, he wrote again: *Perhaps you'll miss him less if you come to visit where he spent the happy days of his childhood, the places he loved so much. I'll take you round myself to show you them.*

And because I had already read the notebooks filled with my father's Orkney memories, I had already decided to come. Ben Gowan had sent me his phone number. I was to call him when I arrived.

But the letters weren't there. I searched, perplexed. It wasn't until I had half-emptied the bag, until I had consoled myself that at least Meggie would get Ben Gowan's number for me, that I found them deeper, among my underthings.

A woman's voice answered the ringing phone, "Pentwater Farm."

My father had never mentioned a Mrs. Gowan, but this must be she.

"Hello. My name is Isabel Garth. I've just arrived from the States. I'd like to speak to Ben Gowan, please."

There was silence. Perhaps the woman hadn't heard, or she wasn't Mrs. Gowan after all. Perhaps I'd done something wrong in dealing with the complications of the coin-operated telephone. I spoke again more carefully, "Hello. May I speak to Ben Gowan, please?"

After another silence there came a reply. "I'm sorry. Ben Gowan is dead."

Four

This guest of summer,
The temple-haunting martlet, does approve
By his loved mansionry that the heaven's breath
Smells wooingly here.
                    —MACBETH, ACT I, SCENE vi

I woke the next morning not knowing where I was, or when, knowing only a familiar ache I thought had gone away. Then I remembered that the ache was grief. Grief, now not for my father, but for his friend, a man I'd never met.

The woman on the phone last night was Ben Gowan's sister. Her brother's illness had begun in the early spring, gone into remission, and then returned. The doctors had said he would die. He and his sister refused to accept that, had fought it, and for a time, won. It must have been in the beginning that he wrote to me of hope. And when his health seemed improved, he must have written his condolences, and his invitation to me. But three weeks ago he had died.

My grief was real, but suffused with disappointment. Ben Gowan had shared my father's childhood. I'd looked forward to his guidance, both to Orkney as it was today and especially to Orkney as it used to be, as it was in my father's notebooks.

I'd found the notebooks soon after my father's death, thick, bound journals detailing his childhood in a crabbed, neat hand. I didn't know when they'd been written—long ago when the memories were fresh and sharp, little by little through the years as they came back to him, or in a secret rush toward the end, when they would have seemed sweeter and their recording more urgent. They told of a boyhood in a place at once familiar and exotic, in a long-ago time not yet completely passed from these remote islands.

I read the notebooks through all those confused days and nights of dealing with my father's death. I read them again soon after, when Allan left me.

When my father died I had grieved deeply, but I rejoiced, too, in my regained freedom. I rejoiced to have my own life again, to go back to my teaching, and to Allan, a fellow teacher. We'd planned to marry. He'd endured with patient grace my dying father's demands on my time and energy, my sometimes threadbare emotional fabric, my final despair. Then, not long after the funeral, he told me he'd fallen in love with someone else.

"But when...how...?" I stuttered.

"At school," he answered, and so great was my confusion that I never asked him who.

He took my face between his hands. "I'm sorry. This surprised me as much as..." As much as you, he meant to say, before he realized how impossible that would be. He kissed my tears away. "I still love you, you know. I always will."

And because I believed that, and could not believe the rest, we made love that night, one last and fateful time.

Then, alone for the first time in my life, frightened and hurt, I resolved to assuage my grief and my anger by editing and publishing the journals. I had come here to illustrate them. And to mourn and celebrate my father's life. Ben Gowan would have helped me. Now he, too, was dead.

Though I didn't know exactly where my father used to live, he'd left me clues enough. That morning, with a map and Meggie's help, I found a cottage, deserted by its look, where a farm track crossed the road. Its surrounding wall had crumbled in places. Broken earth and new stone showed where repairs had been started. Flowers growing from chinks in tumbled rock showed where they had not been continued. Grimy windows swallowed the sun, and weeds thrived in the garden. Tall blue flowers had escaped from the borders and taken over the front path.

But its boxy shape, the twin, multipaned windows on either side of the door, the ochre and sienna chimney pots, fit my father's description of his home here. *Empty still*, he'd written—when?— *save for the mice and birds*. And indeed, a swallow or a swift broke just then from the chimney, and circled upward to become a speck in the sky before disappearing altogether. As a sign, it was insufficient. Besides, I didn't believe in signs.

I was confident enough, though, to make drawings of the house, of its neglected garden, of the wall—especially of the wall. Even if the cottage turned out not to have been my father's, the wall had a moldering beauty of its own that could later become lovely watercolors.

A single car came down the quiet road while I drew, and it turned into the drive to park behind my car.

"What are you doing here?" The driver climbed out, blustering. "Oh, it's you," he said. His churlish look turned more affable. It was Ross, Meggie's friend.

"I'm sorry," I said. "The place seemed deserted. Is it yours? I'm not trespassing, at least not in the house."

He'd come close by then, and looked over my shoulder at my sketchbook. "You've nothing more exotic to draw, in all of Digerness?"

"I think this is where my father once lived."

"Ah," was all he said for a time, then, "Well...I'm fixing it up, but that means tearing it apart first. I've left supplies around, and many things to trip over. You could hurt yourself. Best not to come again."

I had seen a ladder propped around the corner, and a pile of roofing slates near the front door, but nothing lurking dangerously, nothing unavoidable. Still, "I'm sorry," I said again. "I'd been hoping to find the owner, to be allowed to go inside as well."

He had already picked up my sketchbook and pencils, and was guiding me to my car. He opened my door, then closed it behind me and gave a small wave, but he still held my sketchbook. "Oh, your book!" He laughed at his absentmindedness when I asked for it, handing it to me. "Tell you what, come another day. I'll show you round inside. Just call me."

But apparently he wouldn't allow me there on my own. At least I'd got my drawings of the outside.

Even with Ross's interruption, I had almost filled my sketchbook. I detoured on the way back to the village to pull off the road on a hilltop, where I could fill the remaining pages with images of a distant lofty ruin I'd glimpsed against the sky. My father had written of such a spot, a favorite for fantasy play and rowdy games with his friends. This could have been the place.

In the village, just around a corner from the tearoom where I ate my lunch, I found Spindrift, the craft co-op where Johanna's Aunt Nan sold her quilts. The shop was filled with needlework and knitting and jewelry, baskets and Orkney straw chairs. Weavings hung from the walls, bright colors and patterns beckoning, and I thought of Thora with a slight unease.

When I went back to the inn for another sketchbook, Meggie gave me a map marked with symbols of Viking palaces, and Iron Age masonry towers, and standing stone circles. She traced with her finger the road I should take to the stones I'd passed yesterday, the Ring of Brodgar and the Stones of Stenness, and Andrew's errant Watch Stone. She paused at the blue *P* indicating the parking area between the lochs.

"And you'll be visiting Maes Howe as well?" Meggie, taking it for granted that I would, moved her finger along the road and rounded a corner, then added a brochure to those she already held in her other hand.

"I don't think so. Not today."

"But why not?" A faint uncertainty puckered between Meggie's eyebrows. "You'll be right there. You can see the mound from the stone monuments, just across this bit of water. If you see nothing else, you must see Maes Howe. Our most valuable treasure, some folk say." She lifted her voice slightly and recited, "The finest example of prehistoric architecture in Western Europe."

But it was a tomb, and today of all days I had no wish to visit tombs.

In the end I went anyway.

Summer still shone from a blue sky, but the wind at the lochs had a biting edge. Still, families picnicked here and took walks, ignoring the many monuments and looking instead at the boundless landscapes.

The throb of a tractor working a nearby field carried across the treeless moor. A fisherman waded in the shallows of the Loch of Harray, casting his fly onto the choppy surface. A few small boats drifted farther out. Along the shore a line of wooden rowboats, each painted a different color, lay beached on a crescent of sand and grass. I leaned against my car to draw them. These, too, would later become watercolors.

A tour bus from Kirkwall drove up and parked as I crossed the road to the Ring of Brodgar, and its passengers straggled over to join me there.

Heather, its purple buds still tightly closed amid the spiky,

green-brown leaves, spread over the raised earthwork and the surrounding ditch. I followed the foot-worn path inside the circle.
Some of the stones, I knew, were gone. A few were broken, some
lay fallen and scattered. The front had sheared from one, and
yellow lichens grew on the exposed surface. Its cleft face still lay
before it, partly buried, quickly becoming one with the land. Solid
and upright, others loomed over me. From their deep shadowy
bases they thrust jagged, pointed tops to the heavens. Words in
the brochure spoke of measured precision, of the sun, the moon,
and the stars, of sight lines, and ancient rituals. Here stood the
stones themselves, and words for now got in the way.

I sat on a thick slab of stone outside the Ring and drew the
circle. I drew the tiny yellow flowers of a butter-and-eggs that grew
between a monolith and some of its broken fragments.

My father had written how he and his friends, surely Ben
Gowan among them, had once collected such bits of rock from
the site or, perhaps more likely, natural rubble. Whatever their true
source, the boys invented ceremonies around them, until they
frightened themselves with ancient legends and scattered the fragments, for safety, in the churchyard.

It was unlikely that it was on one of these stones that my
father had found the markings. Ben Gowan's last letter to him
before he died, one I had read to him, said: *Remember the markings
you discovered? I found that stone again. It brought me memories, but more,
much more. I must have your advice, but first must think it out.*

Both of them now gone, Ben Gowan would never ask my
father's advice, or mine, or tell me what my father's stone had
brought him. Was it too late for me to find out? Someone else
might know. My father's words, read yet again, or the familiar
places of his childhood, might tell me. I might find them myself.

The wind tore at my pages now, sharper, and smelling of the
sea. I stood and looked around. Far clouds had gathered in. Wind
lines streaked the dark surface of the loch. The families were gone,

and the fisherman, and the boats on the water. Of the bus tour group, only one remained at the monument, a round man wrapped in a heavy, shawl-collared sweater.

Symbols of antiquities densely marked this area of my map. Small mounds surrounded me, and other standing stones bordered the road that ran between the lochs to the Stones of Stenness, a mile distant.

I pulled my jacket tighter and began to walk. Cows in the fields alongside moved to the fence to watch me with broad, placid faces. A large gray hawk sailed low over a pasture. The few houses that lined the road, ordinary houses, seemed unaware of their extraordinary surroundings. Across from one stood the soaring Watch Stone.

A fine mist needled my face. I walked on. I turned back once, to see the round man standing beneath the Watch Stone, tilted back on his heels to take in its full height, his hands thrust into his sweater pockets as if to counterbalance his backward lean. Hunching over my paper, I made a quick drawing of them both.

He caught up with me at the Stones of Stenness. We entered the fenced enclosure separately, not speaking. We found ourselves in a sheep meadow, a half-dozen unshorn sheep grazing among the four stones that were all that still stood in this circle. Clumps of shed fleece littered the grass where we walked. The sheep grazed on, uninterested, moving serenely away when we came too near.

The man cast curious glances at the sketchbook tucked into my coat as our paths crossed at the stones. Finally I held it out for him to see his image dwarfed before the stone three times his size.

He nodded his approval.

"Been here before?" he asked with a New Yorker's voice. His hands still in his pockets, he indicated the whole of Orkney with a slight toss of his head.

"No. In fact, I've just arrived. This is the first site I've visited. Have you?"

"Nope. But my wife, she came here when she was a kid. She's a Scot, you see. Gets homesick sometimes, so we come to Scotland every couple of years to visit the family, and this year we came up here, too." He poked his chin at the evenly contoured, large green hill on the other side of the loch. "That's where we're headed after this. Maes Howe. You, too?"

I shook my head. My father had written about the tomb. It had probably been built by the same people who built these henges, but its purpose was different, dark and hidden, and they had mounded it over with earth and grass. "No, I don't think so."

I must have made a face, given some hint of my aversion, because he quickly put in, "Oh, it's not spooky or anything. There are no bodies, you know. Haven't been for hundreds of years. It's a great place. Beautiful even, my wife says. See you there," he said with a nod, and set off back down the road.

It may have been curiosity that changed my mind, the lure of the imagination still strong from the stone images. More likely it was the prosaic acceptance of the tomb by this cheerful man. I decided to go to Maes Howe.

He waved at me like an old friend when he saw me approach, and his wife gave me a shy smile when I joined their group around the tomb guide.

The guide had already begun his lecture. "The large stone against the wall on your left soon after you enter was used to close off the entry. Notice the size of the slabs that were used for the building." He ducked and entered the low passageway, calling after, "Watch your heads now."

Only when it was too late, when I could no longer back out, did I learn that the long entry passage was just a few feet high. I walked its length in a crouch, aware only that I was walking into an engulfing tomb.

But when I straightened into the tomb itself, I left behind any sense of confinement.

We stood in a square stone room, brightly lit, a white painted ceiling vaulting high above us. Even in its small, primitive simplicity it had more the feeling of a cathedral than a tomb. Was it intentionally symbolic, I wondered, the difficult passage into this space? The artistic surprise that must have greeted primeval mourners could have been intended as a spiritual one for the dead as well—a painful journey through death to a new world, a difficult birth leading to a new life.

The guide pointed out the long stone buttresses that supported each corner, stretching up from the floor to where the ceiling began its gradual inward bend, and the huge horizontal slabs composing the side walls. He encouraged us to look into the vacant, open cells on three sides, where ancient bones once lay.

"Turn and look back," said the guide, "to the way you came in. On Midwinter's Day the setting sun shines through the entryway to light the tomb."

The tomb would have been pitch-dark in Neolithic times— no white paint, no electric bulbs. I tried to imagine, five thousand years ago, a band of men wrapped in sheepskins against the bitter winter wind, prying away the blocking stone, crawling into the blackness of the tomb, huddling there while the sun crept across the floor to light their ceremonies. Or one man alone, perhaps, a high priest gathering or expending his personal magic.

Or was this magic solely for the dead?

The guide said, "No grave-goods were found here when archaeologists excavated the tomb. Archaeologists, though, were not the first."

"The Vikings," someone said.

"Aye. In the twelfth century they broke into this chamber

through the roof, twice we think, and left a record of their presence."

He turned off the overhead lights, and shone his flashlight around, stopping it here and then there so we could see what we had not seen in the wide diffusion of modern lighting. Faint scratched markings, like stick-trees drawn by a child, marched across horizontal slabs and down vertical ones. Like secrets coming to light, more appeared the longer I looked.

"The Vikings carved runes on the walls," said the guide. "Eight-hundred-year-old graffiti, you might say."

"Messages about treasure." It was the round man.

"Aye, they talk about treasure, do the runes. And they tell about themselves, a bit. They talk about the local girls, too—though some would say those and treasures are the same."

Polite laughter went around the group, but my friend persisted. "Did they find treasure?"

The guide shook his head. "The experts don't think so."

"Why not?"

"They don't think the people who built this tomb would have left anything the Vikings considered treasure."

"Gold," someone said.

"Silver," corrected the guide. "They valued silver more, though they liked gold well enough, did the Vikings. Instead of finding treasure here, they left a treasure for us, this grand collection of runic inscriptions. And the pictures, like this mystical beast, which we've taken for our own."

He fixed his light on a contorted, ornate animal scratched into one of the stones. It was a figure I had seen reproduced that morning in Digerness. "The Orkney Dragon," he said.

I started home through a rain that now lashed horizontally. The steely, broken surfaces of the lochs as I passed them looked cold and uninviting. One hapless driver stood by the roadside, peering helplessly into the raised hood of his Land Rover. His dark, dripping hair plastered his head, his wet shirt clung to his back.

Ross. Again.

I pulled over. He leaned into my window and flashed an even white smile at me.

"Isabel. We seem destined to be together today." He clenched his teeth to prevent their chattering, but his smile broadened, reaching his eyes, narrowing them so their intense blue was almost hidden behind black lashed lids. "Until this minute I cursed my luck, but this seems my lucky day. Close your window, you're letting in the rain. I'll go around.

"Sorry about the wet," he said, settling into the passenger seat, "but I'm sure to dry quickly. Turn on the heater, please?"

When we were headed once again toward Digerness, I glanced over at him. He was a different Ross from this morning. He had pushed back his seat and reclined against it, his long legs stretched out and crossed at the ankles. He looked contented and comfortable, and dry. With no more than a toss, his hair had resumed its blow-dry look.

I became aware of my own hair, sopped flat and lifeless by my dash through the rain, and I ran my fingers through it without much hope.

"What have you done since this morning?" he asked after a time. "Are you enjoying yourself?"

"I've been to the standing stones, and to Maes Howe."

"Ah. Did you learn about the treasure, then?"

"I learned that there probably wasn't any. Or if there was, it has already been found."

"Just as well, I suppose," he said, and his tone became flippant. "There's bound to be more somewhere else, don't you think? And without Hogboy to guard it."

"Hogboy?" I knew the legends of the tomb. None of those

stones, discovered and studied by others, were my father's marked stone, but he had spent schoolboy hours trying to decipher what he'd decided were runic clues to a still-existing treasure. Still, Hogboy was something new to me.

"The guides don't tell you everything, do they? Hogboy is a troll who lives in the tomb and guards the treasure. Or used to guard it. If it's not there anymore he didn't do a very good job, did he?"

"What about the Dragon?" I said, getting into the spirit. "I would have thought that the Dragon guards the treasure."

"The Dragon is Viking. Hogboy is older, Pictish. At least I believe so. Don't worry, though," he added quickly, as if I had reacted with some alarm, "since the treasure is gone, Hogboy certainly is, too. No need to guard the bones. Who wants old bones?"

"There aren't any bones," I told him.

"No?" He shrugged and waved his hand, brushing away his ignorance. "Well, then, we can forget about them, can't we? And about graves, too. Have dinner with me tonight."

The sudden memory of his brief closeness yesterday arose, and with it, doubt. Why should he want to have dinner with me? Some men considered me attractive enough, and one, for a time at least, had found me beautiful. Allan had made much of my hazel eyes, my gleaming light brown hair, in lover's praise. But Ross hardly knew me. And at thirty-five I was probably ten years older than he was, older still than the delicate Meggie, with whom he was obviously involved. I looked at him. His face, darkly handsome, gave no hint of his intent.

As though he'd read my thoughts, Ross added, "In gratitude for rescuing me."

He probably turned on the charm for everyone, flirting from nothing more than habit. Inviting me to dinner was a friendly gesture, perhaps an apology for dismissing me from the cottage this morning. Feeling silly for having imagined anything more, I accepted. It would be better than eating alone at the inn.

"Good. I'll take you to O'Hara's."

"O'Hara's?"

"O'Hara's Pub. We're not all Scots here in Orkney, nor Norsemen. They have fine local food, and Irish folksingers as well."

We could hear the noise before we opened the door, the clatter of plates and glasses, the hum of conversation punctuated with laughter, and the music.

I would have guessed from the noise that no one was listening to the music, but as we entered the bar the song ended, and the crowd erupted with cheers and applause. The musicians, visible on their raised platform in the far corner despite the smoky blue haze that filled the room, responded with elaborate bows. As well as smoke, smells filled the air, smells of wet wool, of hot grease, of vinegar and beer, and for just an instant my stomach lurched.

"Come on." Ross grabbed my hand. "If we're lucky we'll get that last table."

He pulled me after him, weaving between close tables, jostling others with apologies, "Sorry—coming through now—sorry, love."

The menu, a blackboard chalked in large white letters, hung high on the wall behind the bar. As I read it, I couldn't help laughing.

"You promised me fine local food," I accused him. The singers had begun again, and I had to raise my voice to be heard above them. "I expected finnan haddie, and haggis at least. This says steak and fish and chips."

"Aye, but Scottish fish and chips," he called back. "Or rather, Orkney fish and chips, better still. And Orkney beef."

He pulled his chair up close and said into my ear, "You'll have your haggis at the inn, I'm bound. If I promised you fine local food here, that's exactly what you'll have. An authentic farmer's tea, his supper, when he doesn't have it at home. The best in the world."

And he was right, at least so far as I could tell. While we ate we listened to the music and watched the musicians. One man played a fiddle, one a guitar, and another a silver flute. Their blousy white shirts, open-necked and roll-sleeved, gave them a slightly piratical air. The lone woman, in a long, moss-green dress, played a lap harp, and sometimes silver spoons, ringing them off her knees and the heels of her hands, her hands dancing in the air in time with the music they themselves had made. The men acted as much as they played and sang, their expressive faces mugging the emotions of the songs.

Watching the musicians, I noticed a man come into the bar, a large, brown man. Brown hair, a brown raincoat open over a brown sweater, and shabby brown corduroys. He stood blocking the light from the doorway, surveying the faces in the room. His eyes met mine and briefly stayed, and then moved on to Ross. He smiled, and pushed his way through the room.

"Hello, Ross," he said. "There doesn't seem to be a place to sit tonight." He took an empty chair from the next table and swung it around to ours. "Mind if I join you?"

He didn't wait for an answer, but sat. Then he stood again, and offered me his hand.

"I don't believe we've met," he said. "I'm Graham Sinclair."

Before I could tell him my name, Ross, in a grudging tone, completed the introduction he hadn't at first offered. "Isabel Garth. She's visiting from America."

Graham waved at our waitress, who seemed to understand this as his order. Then he looked at Ross and me, directing his gaze back and forth between us.

"Family?" he asked. "Or friend?"

"I'm not visiting Ross," I said. "I'm visiting Digerness. I met

Ross yesterday, at the inn. Furrowend. Meggie Denison introduced us."

He raised his eyebrows, and I saw that his eyes, too, were
brown.

"You're staying in Digerness?" He sounded surprised. "What
brought you here?"

I wondered if all Digerness visitors were greeted with such
skeptical curiosity. I answered him the same way I'd answered Ross.

"Your father, I'm certain, never spoke of my museum," Graham
said in response, "but I hope you'll see it anyway."

"Your museum? The Tankerness, you mean, in Kirkwall?"

He laughed, shaking his brown head. "Not so grand as that,
nor so far away. Between here and there. Sinclair House. My family
home, actually. My great-grandfather was eccentric."

"Ach, and rich," Ross grumbled.

Graham continued as though Ross hadn't spoken. "He collected everything, from art and Victorian furniture to old farm
implements. Everything he could find of the Orkney Isles. Some
reproductions, too, I must admit, but informative still. The museum is open to the public in summer, and in the winter I teach
the children. They come to the museum, teachers and students, on
their school outings, from Mainland and the rest of the islands.
They stay for the day. I show them our collections and lecture
them on a wide variety of art and history subjects."

"I'm a teacher, too," I told him. "That is, I've been on leave,
but I'll begin again in the fall. An art teacher, originally, but now
in a general classroom. Twelve-year-olds. I wish I could bring them
here." I smiled at the thought. "What an outing that would be."

"We must see if we can arrange something," Graham said
seriously. "Now, what have you seen so far?"

As I spoke to Graham, I became aware of Ross, left out of
the conversation, making a display of his boredom. He drummed
his fingers against the table and precisely aligned his beer glass

with some imaginary focus. When the musicians reappeared he turned his chair to face them and joined in the enthusiastic applause.

He had a right to sulk. After all, it was he who'd brought me here. Now Graham dominated the evening. I reached for Ross's arm, determined to talk to him as much as to Graham, but before I could the musicians began to play. They'd begun with romantic ballads, soft and lyrical, but now their songs were loud and bawdy, popular with the audience, who sang along at a volume that increased with each new tune. I would have to wait for a chance to mollify Ross.

During the first quiet moment between songs Graham leaned toward me. "If you're interested in the past," he said, "I've several books to recommend. And some to loan. Have you read the *Orkneyinga Saga?* Myth, some of it. But a grand history, even so, of our Viking past. Viking earls ruled here for more than five hundred years, you know."

I nodded. "I know. And I have read it. My father required it. Not that I remember much now, or even absorbed much then. I skipped too many pages, I think. I'll have to read it again."

As the musicians laid down their instruments for a break, Ross said quickly into the silence, "When you bring your students to Orkney you must bring them to my farm. I've a burnt mound you'll no doubt want to see while you're here."

Graham dismissed it. "Stones used by Bronze Age man for cooking, then discarded in a pile. Quite common."

"I've part of the dwelling as well, don't forget. They're not so common as all that."

"A cooking pit only." Graham turned to me. "We have so many antiquities here it's rare for a farm to be without one—a burnt mound, or a burial cist, or even more exciting finds, such as chambered tombs."

"Common or not," I said, not only to make Ross feel better—

I was here partly, after all, to look at stones—"I've never seen one. And I'd like to be shown an ancient site by the person who found it."

"Then you shall," said Ross, his humor restored, "whenever you wish."

Graham looked at his watch. "Isn't it past your bedtime, Ross? I thought farmers got up with the sun and went to bed right after tea."

Replete with the wonders of the day and the pleasures of the evening, I said, "It's past my bedtime, too."

Graham was already beside me, helping me into my jacket. "I'll take you back, Isabel."

"I have my own car. Perhaps you'll take Ross home." Going home together would serve them both right for behaving so childishly, "His car's broken down on the road."

One of the players plucked his strings to signal the music would begin again. At the stage I glimpsed someone with wild red hair whisper to the harpist before disappearing into the crowd.

The band began an unfamiliar song, a sad one, I gathered, though at first I paid no attention to the words. No matter what the words, the Irish voices wrung every drop of teary sentiment from them. The lead singer stood with his head bowed, his eyes closed, his fist over his heart beating the rhythm lightly against his chest.

O'Hara's patrons, a spirited audience, listened, learned, and soon were joining in. Even the waitress, collecting payment, tried to hum the tune. The last chorus, with everyone finally singing along, followed us out the door, and boisterous though it now was, each word rang clear in the fresh, rain-washed air.

Go careful, stranger, through the glen,
Go careful up the brae,

The heather or the boggy fen
May steal your life away.

There must have been hundreds of redheads in Orkney, in Digerness, but I had recognized Thora with the musicians. Had she been asking for this song? For me? It might have been about a clan war, or possibly even about a visit to Scotland captivating, possessing one's soul. What nonsense to see a parallel, to imagine that the song held a meaning, a message for me, like Thora's dire warning on the Stromness pier. But I felt sick again all the same, and suddenly I wanted to be at home, in my own house, in my own bed. Not on a foreign shore.

I'd intended to fall into bed, to bury myself beneath the quilt. But three of my father's notebooks sat on the dresser not exactly where I'd left them, and the filled sketchbook I'd placed beside them was gone.

I looked everywhere, even under the dresser and under the bed, before I went downstairs to Meggie.

"Someone's been in my room," I told her. "My books are moved..."

"The maid," she put in quickly, hopefully.

I shook my head. "My sketchbook is gone."

A look close to panic crossed her face. "Are you sure?" she asked, and almost immediately turned and called, "Dad."

Her father appeared at once. I'd noticed both her parents in the restaurant. Ivor Denison, fairer still than Meggie, and tall, with close-cropped, bristled hair, held himself erect. The small round lenses of his eyeglasses added to his air of stern authority. The inn may have been Meggie's responsibility, but he apparently kept close watch. He knew my name.

"A problem, Miss Garth?"

He listened, showing none of Meggie's emotions, and when I finished said, "Upsetting, I can see. But we've no thieves here, understand, not of books nor anything else. We'll find your book," he said, "lost or mislaid."

He gave the last remark like an order, and having issued it, he turned and was gone.

Five

He did command me to call timely on him
—MACBETH, ACT II, SCENE iii

The way to Ben Gowan's farm began as did the way to my father's cottage, past tall, overgrown meadows where here and there a red-billed oystercatcher stood guard over them from atop a fence post. The gravestone-like posts sprang up more abundantly here. Had I seen them last night they might have loomed in my dreams, inscribed with my name, or my father's and Ben Gowan's, or marked in some indecipherable way like the stone both men had found.

But my sketchbook had been discovered this morning shelved with other books in the guests' lounge at the top of the stairs. "You must have dropped it passing through," Meggie said. "Someone found it, and thought it belonged to the inn." So though I was certain I'd placed it on my dresser beside the other books, I was as eager to accept an innocent explanation as Meggie was to give one, and last night's alarms had burned off like fog in the bright glare of the morning sun.

* * *

At a crossroads not far beyond the cottage three arrows
pointed to three farms, and for a moment I could not remember
the name Ben Gowan's sister had given to his farm when two
nights ago she had agreed, reluctantly it had seemed to me, to my
visit.

"Pentwater," said one of the signs, jogging my memory. I followed its arrow shape to the left.

At the low, pebbled house at the end of the lane a woman
stood in the open door, her hand shielding her eyes from the
sunshine as she watched me walk up the path.

"You'll be the Garth lass."

I nodded. "Isabel." I put out my hand. "Miss Gowan?"

"Mrs. MacDonald," she said. "Bea MacDonald. Come in to
the parlor." She pushed her back against the door and led me into
the house.

"I've the kettle on for tea," she said when we sat facing each
other on an orange-patterned sofa and chair. The carpet was of a
different pattern, but as brightly colored. A cabinet stood against
one wall, floral china balanced neatly behind the glass front. A
yellow-tiled fireplace was at another. But despite the glaring colors,
the room was plain.

Bea MacDonald, too, was plain. The unrelieved black of her
dress would be mourning, of course, but it seemed to suit her, as
though she wore it all the time. Her eyes were black, too, haloed
with purple shadows. Her hands, clasped tightly in her lap, were
knobby and misshapen. She must have been sixty, or more than
that, but her hair, smoothed back into a tight bun, shone like a
black cap, with not a hint of gray.

"We've no sherry," she said. Her mouth was a thin, uncom-
promising line. "I don't abide with spirits."

"Tea will be very nice," I said, though I wanted neither sherry nor tea. After Ben Gowan's letters, his friendly invitation, I hadn't expected this stiff, dour woman. I'd hoped to ask about her brother's find, but knew now she'd tell me nothing, if she knew. I said awkwardly, "I've come to tell you I'm sorry about your brother's death. His friendship meant a lot to my father, and his letters were a great comfort to me."

She ducked her head with a murmured response, then looked up at me, her black eyes narrowed. "You were in correspondence with my brother?" Her tone was accusing.

"My father was. They wrote regularly. They were childhood friends, you see, and the friendship lasted to the end." She must have known, and since she, too, had grown up here, she must have known my father as well. "Callum Garth was my father."

Bea MacDonald nodded. "Aye, I mind Callum Garth. Though I was but a wee lass when he left, I mind him well enough. And I know he wrote to my brother. Ben showed me the letters sometimes. Interesting, they were, about life in America." She looked down at her shoes, black and shiny as her hair, and her face softened. "I'm sorry," she said, "sorry for your own loss."

When she looked up again her lips were tightly drawn, though the softness remained around her eyes.

But the softness didn't last. Her tone was severe as she said, "You wrote to my brother yourself."

"Yes. I wrote to him about my father—about his final illness, and then again about his death. Your brother invited me here." She must have known that. I waited a minute before repeating, "Your brother's replies were very comforting. Would you like to read them?"

"Aye." She took my letters and read without comment. When she finished she let them fall into her lap, and she stared past me with unfocused eyes.

"He was a good man, my brother," she said presently. "A godly man. He took us in when we lost my man, Fergus, me with my wee bairn too late in life. Ben never married, never needed to. I did everything for him, cared for him, cooked his meals, and kept this house for him. And he treated my son as his own, he did, let him work alongside him as a lad, taught him to be a good farmer like himself. The farm belongs to us now, to me and my son." She closed her eyes and shook her head. "He was a good man," she said, "even—" She opened her eyes and looked at me. "Aye, he was a good man."

This seemed, for Bea MacDonald, to be an open declaration of sorrow, as close as she would come to sharing grief. She handed back the letters. "That's my brother, there on the mantel."

Nothing was out of place in this spare, tidy room, no open books face down on tables, nothing used and set aside, nothing personal except this, a photograph in a gold-colored frame, set slightly askew on the mantelpiece.

I was glad of a chance to move. I picked up the frame. The photograph was of a man standing beside a wall, holding his hat in his hand, wiping his brow with his forearm. Much of his face lay in shadow, except for the broad white smile. He was dark, like his sister, but he was tall, and held himself with an easy, familiar grace. I didn't remember my father having a picture of him, but I felt I'd seen Ben Gowan before. As the reason for this occurred to me, I heard someone come into the house.

"My son," said Bea MacDonald. She rose quickly, smoothing her skirt, and started for the hall. Before she reached it he appeared in the archway, completely at ease in this spotless room in his coveralls and Wellington boots.

"Isabel!" said Ross MacDonald. "What a grand surprise. I didn't expect to see you so soon, but I'm glad. You've come to see my burnt mound, I suppose."

"I've come to offer my condolences to your mother."

"For Uncle Ben. Aye." He laid his arm lightly across his

mother's shoulders. Her dour countenance melted. She relaxed against him, her head against his chest.

"We miss him, don't we, Mam?" he said to her, and he put his hand to her cheek in a tender gesture. Then his bright smile flashed. "Am I just in time for tea, then?" he said, teasing.

Bea MacDonald straightened, and her black eyes blazed at him. "You'll no step into my parlor wearing those boots," she said, and she marched out past him to bring in the tea.

"Now then," Ross said after we'd finished the tea, the thick-sliced sandwiches, the squares of raisin cake. He put his hands on his knees. "We'll walk out to see my burnt mound, shall we?"

His mother paused in stacking cups and saucers on a tray. "She's no prepared for tramping in the fens."

His eyes ranged over the skirt and sandals I'd brought with me for Sundays, came up to my eyes, and winked. "She'll do," he said.

"The walk's an easy one," he told me. "You'll have no difficulties, I think."

"Your mother is right, I'm not prepared. Another day, I hope. But I could walk to the cottage—"

"The cottage?" Bea interrupted.

"It used to be her father's," Ross said, though she can't have needed that explanation. "She'd like to look through it." He gave it some thought. "Oh, all right, we'll go," he said to me. "But not for long."

"Her bonny dress—" objected Bea, but she said no more.

Ross was right when he'd said he was tearing the cottage apart. In the front hall, lath was exposed where walls had been ripped. Doors had been removed from their jambs. Lumber lay along the stairs, and through the open door of the cubbyhole cupboard under the stairs, I saw paint cans stacked. In the next room plasterboard leaned against the walls. White dust filmed everything.

There were only two rooms on the main floor—the parlor on one side of the hall, and the kitchen on the other. The parlor was bare except for a brick fireplace with a black iron sconce on either side. A fireplace was in the kitchen, too, and a deep-welled sink, and a built-in cupboard like the one under the stairs. I stood in the center of the room and tried to picture a table, my young father and his parents around it, amid warmth and steam and hearty smells.

"I'd like to go upstairs alone," I told Ross.

As I made my way past the stacked wood, I imagined Callum the boy, with a sun-reddened face and pockets full of pebbles and seashells, climbing up to bed. His bedroom would have been the smaller of the two, above the kitchen. His bed would have tucked under the steep slope of the roof, a small dresser, perhaps, in the shadows at the far end of the room. The wide sill of the dormer window would have served as the treasure house for his nature collections. He would have had them then, I knew, for he had them his life long.

I forced the window up a few inches and laid my arms on the sill, staring out at my father's view, which did not quite reach the sea. Unconsciously I reached for my sketchbook, but what I wanted to do now was not to draw, but to write. I wanted to write a letter to my father, to tell him I was here.

Perhaps he knew. I sat in the dust on the floor and cried.

Ross waited for me at the bottom of the stairs, but came up to meet me when I reached the lumber stack. He took my hand, and put an arm lightly around my waist. "Careful, now, don't fall."

I'd needed no help, and might more easily have fallen because of him. The stairway, laden as it was, had no room for both of us. I pulled away, and raced down the stairs ahead of him, and out.

As we walked away from the cottage, an awkward silence between us, I saw a familiar dark green car out of the corner of my eye, speeding down the farm track.

"Where does that road go?" I asked, to fill the empty air.

He shrugged. "Nowhere, really. A croft-road, for tractors and such."

I'd recognized the car, or thought I had.

"Thora," I said.

Ross looked sharply at me. "So you know Thora, too, do you?" His voice had an edge to it. "Isn't it wonderful how you've managed? You've been here only a few days and already you know half the parish."

"We met in Stromness, on the pier. She was on the *St. Ola,* too, the day I arrived."

I said no more. It was none of his affair how we'd met, or the danger Thora had predicted for me. Danger? Fate, or Thora herself, perhaps, had better get to work. I laughed.

Ross gave me another sharp look, but I just smiled at him. I didn't explain.

Six

We have met with foes
That strike beside us.
—MACBETH, ACT V, SCENE vii

Be careful what you wish for. The Irish singers should have
sung that to me.

I collected my car from Bea MacDonald's yard and drove it
back to the inn so I could walk around the village, to record what
remained there of my father's memories. After sketching a shop
where he'd spent rare pennies for candy, I had only the harbor to
draw, where the masts of the boats waiting to sail away marked a
rhythmic pattern against the clear sky. Behind them crouched the
hazy blue hills of a far island that must have called to him. Here
he'd dreamed of piracy, of running off to sea.

Only a few people shared the street leading down to the harbor
with me, late shoppers rushing home to their dinners. As I passed
a narrow passageway connecting this street with some other, or
with a hidden close, someone exploded out of it, flying into me,
and sending me into flight as well. I landed on my knees on the
curb, and still moving, bumped off it and skidded into the street.

"Oh my," someone said, "Are you hurt, my dear?"

One of the shoppers had come to my rescue. I knew it was not my assailant. Assailant, because I had felt hands flat against my back before I fell.

The woman helped me to sit, and wiped at the blood and grit on my knees with a large, white handkerchief.

"I saw the whole thing," she said, after assuring herself that bumps and scrapes were the worst of my injuries. "These young hooligans. Own the world, they think, and in a hurry with it. Don't get in the way!"

"Did you see who . . . ?"

"I did." Another shopper had joined us. "Tall, and all in black," she said. "Black hair, besides."

"That was his hat," the first one said. "His hat was black. Not so tall as all that, and his hair was red."

Both women, arguing amiably, helped me home, and Meggie made a fuss, cleaning my wounds and icing my left knee, which had begun to puff.

She brought dinner to my room, but I had lost my appetite. Propped against my pillow, I leafed back through my filled sketchbook. I found tiny scraps of torn paper left tangled in the spirals, and could not find all the drawings. Those of the wall surrounding my father's cottage and the ruin standing against the sky had been ripped from my book.

"Someone liked them," Meggie said, after I'd called her back to my room. "A guest, when the book was lost. Saw them, and took them. They do, you know, no matter what my father says. They cut recipes from magazines, take home our scenic photo books. Even towels, do you believe?"

I did believe. Why else would my pictures be gone?

Seven

Your hand, your tongue: look like th' innocent flower,
But be the serpent under't.

—MACBETH, ACT I, SCENE V

Sunday morning, feeling better, I went to my father's church. The road to St. Anne's was narrower even than the farm lane beside his house, all overgrown and hedged in with flourishing crops. I worried that I was on the wrong road, that this was not a proper road at all, that it would lead me, at the end, straight into a barn or milking shed. My worry changed to virtual certainty when I came upon two goats tethered to a gate, standing by the wayside like a pair of rustic hitchhikers.

But the road, despite its little-used, pastoral air, was right, and I wound up after all at St. Anne's. I parked in the mown plot in front of the churchyard and followed other worshipers to the church door, wending my way with them on a grassy path between old tombstones. The watching stone faces of the angels had been scoured and rounded by time. The chiseled names and dates, though legible to those who cared to read them, had softened, too, giving me pause, reminding me that time would do the same for my own loss and grief.

I ducked through the low doorway, and slid into the next-to-last pew, looking about at the humble sanctuary with the same curiosity as I'd looked at my father's house.

I saw no cross, no symbols or decorations save for a few simple carvings on the plain wooden expanse of the paneled wall at the front of the church, and on the lectern. Tall windows in either end of the long building, clear but for four fiery red top panes, expressed the same quiet abandon. It was as though, constrained to simplicity, the workmen had finally surrendered, in this small way, to their joy.

The pews filled. The electronic organ, pipeless and as simple as everything else in the church, played. We stood to sing a hymn, and as it ended a small group of people came forward: two couples, a small girl, and a baby. Parents and sister, godparents, and child. I had come here for solace; instead, I would witness a christening.

I sat, my back held ramrod straight by the shallow, upright pew. Cold radiated from the thick stone wall beside me, and, I thought, from deep within me. Heavy with all the symptoms, I was sure now I was pregnant, and not at all sure of what to do. I pressed my hand against the flatness of my stomach and prayed, though I could not be sure for what.

We stood once more for a hymn, and again, it seemed, at every pause in the service, between each reading of the Scriptures. I sang along with the congregation, following the tunes as well as I could, reading the poetic words in the small red hymnal. I looked up as I sang the words of a psalm set to music.

> For thou, O Lord, hast made me
> Glad by thy work;
> At the works of thy hands
> I sing for joy.

The words belonged to this church, to the wood carvings, and to the red windows. They so nearly reflected my earlier thoughts that as I sang them they became true for me, as once they must have been for the forgotten workmen. Made newly glad, I was ready to seek what my father's journals had told me I might find. No one could see my fingers, hidden by the open hymnal on my lap, search near where a boy had often sat, bored and restless. Before the service ended I found his initials carved in the oak. I traced their shaky, inexpert curves. *C.G.*, they read. Callum Garth, my father. I smiled.

After the service we walked out into the sunshine. The parish children, released from pious stillness, laughed and chased among the graves. It occurred to me then that someday I'd like to have children laughing on my grave.

I walked into the inn that early afternoon, and came to a standstill. From behind Meggie's desk Thora gazed up at me.

"Should you need anything, you must see Meggie," she said curtly, as though we'd never met, as though we had no history. Certainly as though she had not slammed me into the street the day before. She turned away and began tapping at the computer keyboard.

Confounded, I wasn't ready to challenge her. But I did question Meggie.

"She comes each Sunday afternoon," Meggie told me. "She uses my computer to keep her records, of shows and sales and such, and for e-mail. In exchange, she sometimes works for me."

"Dusting, making beds?"

"Oh, no," she said. "Here, at the desk."

Still, Thora might have access to the rooms. But even if, as I suspected, she were staging some prophetic demonstration, auguries of danger, herself assuring their fulfillment, what could she want with my drawings?

Perhaps because of Thora's presence that afternoon my injuries seemed to sting and throb with renewed intensity. I finished the harbor drawings I had not done yesterday, then sat in the inn garden to search my father's notebooks once again for some telling words about his marked stone. I found nothing, but read again of the times he'd spent at the ruin on the hill—which hill could it be but the one I'd drawn from afar, the one missing from my book? I could go there. Meggie could tell me what it was, and how to reach it.

Heading around to the front door of the inn, I stopped myself in time to keep from meeting Thora coming out. She was making a show of loud good-byes and thank-yous to someone I couldn't see. As I backed around the corner I heard her whisper, "Tomorrow?" and caught a few snatches of the reply, "... Gallery ... Hepworth."

I could supply the missing words. The Pier Gallery, at the Pier Art Center in Stromness. Barbara Hepworth, a noted British sculptor. Thora would secretly meet someone there tomorrow, among the Hepworth sculptures. I would be there, too.

"A ruin on a hill?" Meggie said. "Hamehollow, that would be. An ancient manor built on one of our highest hills."

I wanted to go after dinner, for the view, I told her. Would that be too late?

"Oh no, 'tis not too late to go about," said Meggie, "and Hamehollow will be grand then. You'll see for miles, and since dark won't come yet for quite a spell, you'll see a lovely sunset the while.

"And you can drive there, almost all the way. The track may be rather rough, mind, and there's a bit of a climb at the end, but I'll give you a walking stick. You'll have no trouble. 'Tis lonely there, and quiet." The glow of her cheeks deepened. "The place is favored by courting couples," she said, "but not on Sunday. They'll no go there on a Sunday."

Getting there proved not as easy as Meggie had promised. The road narrowed as it climbed, grass and clover sprouted in its middle, and tire lanes soon deteriorated into ruts. I bumped over holes and rocks, glad to reach its end, glad to leave the car in the graveled parking lot terraced into the side of the hill.

But the footpath climbed an even steeper grade. I cautiously picked my way up. The smooth knob of the walking stick fit precisely into my palm, giving confidence to my step. When I stopped to rest I looked down on the lesser hills rolling away. Pastures, still dotted at this hour with grazing cattle, faded gradually into the distance.

Hamehollow sat on the hilltop, a shattered rectangle of blue-shadowed, dun-colored stone. A gable end and its chimney remained intact, and the far wall nearly so. A window broke through it, the low western sun shining through its unglazed aperture. A linteled doorway led its extravagant way through a fragmentary wall. Of the other gable end there was little sign, except for a few small heaps of decayed masonry. Flagstones paved parts of the floor, moss and heather carpeted the rest. The whole of the building lay open to the sky.

So many stones. Of all of the details my father had written, why hadn't he written of the stone he found, the stone Ben Gowan had seen again so many years later, and recognized? It was useless for me to search without knowing more. I sat with my back against the far wall and began to draw.

The sky had gone from blue to yellow, then back again to a deeper blue. Now, with the sun dropping below the horizon, thin purple clouds streaked the orange afterglow. In the distance shadows lengthened and deepened, while in the sky above me the blue remained.

Far off, amid its own green meadows, stood the pointed outline of St. Anne's. I could see Digerness, too, the shapes of its roofs and chimneys black against the shimmery background of the sea. No stars twinkled in the radiant Orkney summer sky. Instead, seen from Hamehollow, the lights of the village appeared like stars, one by one in the dusk. The *simmer dim*, my father had called the summer night, when darkness approached with midnight, and then not fully so, and faded into morning after only a few hours.

Above the whistle of the wind came the thin reedy cry of a night bird far away, and nearby something rustled through the grass. The tangy-sweet smells of hay and clover carried through the air. The wall at my back still radiated warmth from the sun.

The sound of a car broke my peace. I heard it labor up the hill and then stop, to be replaced by footsteps crunching over the gravel. Courting couples after all, on a Sunday. I laid my sketchbook beside me and got up, preparing to leave, but it wasn't courting couples. It was Ross.

"Our meeting isn't a coincidence this time," he confessed. "This time I've searched you out. I heard you had an accident. I've been worrying, imagining you an invalid, laid up for days. But when I called for you at the inn I found you gone. Meggie told me you were here."

"An invalid?" I laughed. "A few scrapes. I'm fine now." I was glad to see him. Except for Bea MacDonald, he was the most likely person to know what his uncle had found. I intended to ask.

"I wonder why you would come up here," Ross was saying, twisting slowly, looking around as though he'd never seen the place, stretching his arms out to the desolate ruin, to the emptiness around it. The ruin itself showed cool and pale in the still-fading light, but its shadows reached out to band the hilltop with darkness.

"Meggie told me how to get here. This is a perfect place to enjoy the evening, isn't it? Quiet, with a view of the village. A short walk, just a bit of a climb. She even gave me a walking stick, look."

He looked, instead, at my sketchbook, on the ground where I'd left it. "Ah, more drawing, I see," he said, and picked it up. He skimmed through the drawings of sunset, of faraway Digerness, of the diminishing hills and the sea beyond, and lingered finally over those of the ruin itself.

"Right good!" He gave me an admiring glance, then a frown. "But see here," he said, "you're hurt. Shouldn't you be sitting down?" He found a low level stretch of wall for me, and angled himself against a higher one.

"There's something you might tell me," I began. Ross still held my sketchbook, as he had done at the cottage. He hadn't wanted me there, at least not on my own, drawing. Could my drawings of it have been what he objected to, for some incomprehensible reason? He might somehow have been the one who had taken those few. Belatedly disposed to caution, I asked instead, "Meggie told me this was called Hamehollow, but why, when it's high on a hill?"

"Because the word isn't *hollow* at all, but a corruption of *hallowed*, or *holy*. 'Twas a house at one time, in the sixteenth century, I believe, falling down around itself as it's doing now. When the owner decided to repair it, he discovered that one of the walls was part of an old church. A Norse church, twelfth century, built by one of the Viking earls. Though how the man could tell all this, I'm sure I don't know."

"But what became of it? So much seems to be missing."

"For years folk have taken stones for building, repairing their own walls. And yet today. Look there."

Even in the encroaching dark we could see bare clods of earth and gaps where floor slates once lay. "We've plenty of stone around without coming here for it. If we've nothing else in Orkney we have that."

He began pacing, stopping now and then to tug at the top course of the wall until finally, in a shower of mortar dust, he dislodged a building stone. Then he dropped it, dismissively.

"They long ago took off the roof, in case it should come down on the head of an innocent tourist. If you ask me they should now take the whole thing down. 'Tis a dangerous place. I'm surprised someone hasn't already been struck by a falling rock, or fallen himself to his death."

For one who believed that, he seemed in little hurry to leave. He poked with his toe in the thick growth and raked over the broken ground with the edge of his shoe. He grabbed up a handful of shards, and skimmed them one by one down the hill. I heard them hit and scatter on, sending back tinny echoes of their descent.

He turned back, and when he was just outside the ruined doorway he bent down, and raised up with a white-flowered spike in his hand. He bowed, a mocking, courtly bow, and offered it out to me.

"White heather," he said. " 'Tis said to be good luck. All Scottish brides carry it. Keep it. Put it in your pocket. Or better..." He had moved behind me and stood close, one hand on my shoulder. He reached around in front of me with his other hand, encircling me, turning me within his arms, and tucked the flower behind my ear. I could smell it, its scent mingling with the heady floral air, and beneath it, like the base of an exotic perfume, the smell of Ross.

He was too close.

"I don't think I'll be needing that." I laughed, and reached up to take it away, but he caught my hand and bent closer. His eyes seemed almost black in the deepening gloom.

"And why not?" he said. His accent became thicker, his words more lilting, slipping into the local dialect, as though he was losing himself in my thrall. "Ach, thoo'd be a right bonny bride, I'd not mind to be wed in the kirk to thee myself."

I felt the flower slip from my ear. Ross stepped nearer still.

"Isabel," he whispered, "Belle, my Belle." He let go of my hand and placed his forefinger on my lips, as though marking his target. Then he kissed me, slowly, expertly, moving from my lips to my throat and back again to my lips, murmuring as he did so with words I didn't understand—Gaelic, or Norse, or nonsense perhaps—but the words didn't matter, only his voice, and the rough caress of his tongue, and his hands. While one cradled my head, fingers tangled in my hair, the other, displaced from my lips by his own, traced a path down my throat to the hollow at its base. And from there it barely had to move before recontouring itself into a curve around my breast.

If there had been a fumble, a target missed, a wrong note in the artful island melody he whispered to me, despite my distrust of him I might have succumbed further. If even the rhythm of his heart had quickened; but I could feel its stolid, steady beat against my breast in counterpoint with my own racing heart. Ross's skill betrayed him, and I pulled myself away.

"No, Ross. Don't be silly."

He reared back, affronted. "Silly, am I? Mad, more like!"

He was still close. I was still half wrapped in his embrace. His hands held me there, his strong fingers digging into my shoulders, bruising. Then he gave me a sharp push.

I stumbled back, twisting my still-tender knee. I cried out, startled more by this sudden violence than by any real pain. I expected remorse then, and lavish apologies, but he was gone, stomping down the hillside like a pouting child.

Had he never been rejected before? And he'd only been pretending, after all. He was well aware of his charms. He'd been turning them on in some kind of game since we'd met, I was sure of that now. And I'd responded at last, only to be left feeling shameful and hurt.

I sank to the grass, cradling my knee, exploring for further injury. I was almost disappointed to find none, as if I needed something more tangible than his childish conceit on which to base my anger with Ross. I sat there, waiting to hear the fierce slam of his car door, the roar of his engine as he shot away. But there was nothing except the wind, and the soft sounds of the night.

Long minutes passed. Then, instead of a slam I heard a gentle thump, an engine purring to life, and the slow crunch of tires in their deliberate maneuvering down the rough track.

As I pushed myself up I saw the little sprig of white heather gleaming in the near-darkness, lying limp and flat in the grass beside my hand. I picked it up and regarded it. Good luck for Scottish brides, was it? Ross's flattery aside, I'd never be a Scottish bride, nor, probably, any bride. But I was good enough to wear this flower. In a gesture of bravado I tucked it back behind my ear, and held it there as I walked down the hill to my car.

Eight

There is none but he
Whose being I do fear.
　　　—MACBETH, ACT III, SCENE i

I didn't want to face Meggie in the morning. I remembered how she'd reddened when she'd told me courting couples frequented Hamehollow. She'd gone there herself with Ross. Last night she sent me there, then innocently sent Ross after me. Ross had betrayed her, and though I had resisted at the last, it hadn't been for Meggie's sake. I had betrayed her, too.

I made tea in my room, and slipped out of the inn without breakfast. I could find the Pier Gallery on my own.

I would have gone there in any circumstance, even without Thora, without my need to know what she might be up to. A visit to the Gallery might alone have brought me to Orkney. That small works of Britain's major contemporary artists should be here, in this seaside village, in this far-flung waterfront on the edge of the world, intrigued me.

I parked near the ferry terminal, perhaps at the very spot where I had first met Thora. I watched the waves break into spume against the Art Center's stone pier nearby. I could feel the salt mist on my face, taste the flavor of the ocean on my lips.

On Victoria Street, the iron-railed gate to the Gallery was still shut. Across the street a crowded shop window, crammed with woolly scarves and sweaters, with framed paintings, tiny ship models, and ceramic sheep, caught my eye. I peered around its holdings to see a studio rather than a shop, with stained worktables and sinks, and mayonnaise jars holding up-ended paintbrushes. Children, most of them ten or so, I guessed, hunched over projects. They were needle-weaving bright creations on small cardboard looms. I thought of Andrew, and looked for him, not really expecting to see him there. The teacher came into sight, hurrying to a child's side. It was Thora.

I watched for a while. Amid a chaos of yarn scraps and seashells and other oddments, the children worked mostly on their own. Thora moved among them, crouched beside them, offered them help, and, by the looks of them, rewarded them with sufficient praise. This was a different Thora. This was Thora the teacher, in her everyday world. Thora where she belonged, and had every right to be.

Slightly abashed, I turned back to the Gallery gate. Open now, it led me into a flagged courtyard formed by its buildings, by an ivied wall, by the sea, and centered by a pedestaled green-stained sculpture by Barbara Hepworth.

I wandered through the Gallery's groundfloor rooms, and climbed the stairs to the narrow white attic space. At the top of the stairs a long window framed a view, forcing me to look down at the sculpture I'd just left outside.

I looked at all the art, at the Nicholsons and Wallises, at the Hiltons and Herons, but my concentration wavered, my eyes wandered as much as I did. Hepworth's sculptures stood here and there, her paintings hung among the others, with no hiding place for me. I considered leaving before the class across the street finished, before Thora could come to her meeting place, by whichever work it was, only to find me there.

Through a door with a poem about the sea imprinted on its glass, I looked out at the sea. But I kept coming back to the long window at the head of the stair, to the courtyard, to the one place Thora must have referred to, to the sculpture below. As I stood watching Thora came running into view, to kiss the man who now waited for her there.

The man pulled away hurriedly, not as though her kiss had been unwelcome, or even unfamiliar, but as though it might have been rash. He looked hastily around him, and his eyes swept upward, and Ivor Denison stared into my eyes.

I fumbled for my car keys, and fumbled again getting into the car. Before I closed the door, someone came up from behind, leaned over into the car, and said, "You will say nothing of this. To my wife, to my daughter, Meggie. To no one. Even to *her*. Understand?"

I didn't turn toward him. I nodded, bobbing my head like a shorebird, started my car, and drove away, still nodding. I cursed myself for coming here, for my arrogance, for believing that all of Thora's actions might relate to me.

I didn't want to know what I had learned.

I raced south, across those few islands linked by a causeway, across Holm Sound, past the rusted hulks of World War I battleships that rose out of the shallow waters. Ivor Denison's car stayed close behind.

Finally, when we reached the island of South Ronaldsay, he turned off. Shaking, I drove on to the village of St. Margaret's Hope, where I found a beach to comb, to calm myself. Carrying a brown paper bag of bread and cheese for my lunch, I walked the sand. My mind let go of one worry, only to grab at another.

Ahead of me, a curlew squawked and circled, and flew to its retreat beyond the dunes. A sanderling raced before the edges of the waves, probing the moist sand with its black bill.

I followed the waving line of detritus banked by the tides, and tried to think of nothing but birds and shells and mermaids' purses. Did Orkney children call them mermaids' purses, these leathery black, spur-cornered egg cases of the skate? My only clear memory of my mother, who died when I was five, was of the two of us holding hands on a beach somewhere, surveying our similar day's bounty with mutual congratulations. I wondered about some-day bringing my own child here to find such treasures left on the shore by the ebbing tide, but couldn't imagine it. All ages of women, married or single, seemed to have children these days. But alone, in my mid-thirties, with a newfound freedom beckoning in my future, the prospect dismayed and terrified me. Would I learn to embrace my pregnancy, and see it through? Or would I end it? Both solutions filled me with dread. Perhaps at home I'd find advice. Perhaps that was the answer. Go home.

Thora's advice.

But home today was Digerness, and the inn.

On the way back to Digerness I recognized a road entrance as leading to the way John Rousay had driven us that first day here. Its prospect seemed friendly and familiar, as though I'd trav-eled it many times before, and I turned into it.

Halfway into the journey, my car crested a hill just as a belch-ing tractor lurched out from a farm gate in the valley and crabbed slowly down the road ahead of me, leaving behind a trail of muddy herringbones on the pavement. It cast off bits of straw into the wind; they eddied in the air until they met my car with a slap against the windshield.

I touched the brake lightly, to maintain the distance between us. My car did not slow. I braked again. The pedal went to the floor, offering no resistance. I was gaining momentum, closing the distance at an alarming rate.

The tractor puffed out black exhaust and chugged along, unaware that I charged up behind.

A car approached from the opposite direction, and as it flashed by, another appeared.

I could see the farmer's hat now, bobbing innocently ahead. I could see corroded spots on the wings over the tractor's tires where rust had bitten into the red paint. I could see the detailed pattern of the tire treads as I came ever nearer.

As soon as the approaching car went by, I had intended to pass, to curve to the right around the tractor. Instead, in near-panic, my body acting on its on, I pulled automatically to the left. Toward me now came a field of yellow stubble, strewn with its harvest of round bales, and a fence, and only a strip of grass between it and me. I jerked the car straight. It careened along, partly on the narrow shoulder, partly on the road.

I switched off the ignition.

Immediately I discovered my mistake. I clutched the steering wheel to make sure the car, its power steering switched off with the key, kept going forward as it bumped slowly to a stop.

But before that could happen I hit a shallow ditch, its grass still wet with morning rain. It pulled me in. The wheel wrenched itself from my grasp. The left fender scraped along a wire fence. The car slammed to a stop against a fence post. I had a jarring instant to be grateful that the post was wood, and not, like half the posts in Orkney, a pillar of stone. Then the post cracked and leaned, pulling those on either side into drunken cants. I heard a snap, then a whining *zing*. A single strand of barbed wire whipped into the air, lashed down again, and coiled itself across the hood of my car.

I unclenched my teeth and blew out my breath, only now aware I'd been holding it. My hands and my knees trembled. I pried my fingers from the wheel, swiped my sweating palms across my jeans, and reached up to massage my neck.

As soon as I moved, nausea engulfed me. I closed my eyes and lay back against the seat. That didn't help. I concentrated on breathing in, on gulping down the sweet air, on the breeze cooling my face. I didn't hear someone's car drive up and park behind me. I did hear its door slam and my own jerk open, but I didn't open my eyes until someone laid two fingers on the side of my neck.

Someone was checking my pulse to see if I was dead.

Graham Sinclair's large form filled the doorway. "Are you hurt?" he asked.

When I shook my head it began to spin, as did the earth and Graham's face. His voice sounded ringing and far away. "Don't move just yet," he said. "Sit still a while."

But I couldn't. I pushed past him out of the car. He tried to put an arm around me, but I slid away to kneel in the fence-row.

He stayed beside me. He was there, holding me, when I vomited into the tall grass. He handed me a handkerchief and rubbed my back. I was tempted to stay there, hunched over, being comforted. I didn't want to look at him, to see his face, or especially to let him see mine.

I had no choice. When I straightened he put a hand under my chin and turned me toward him. He wiped my hair back from my damp forehead. "Let's go sit down," he said.

I sat sideways in the open car, my knees drawn up, my hands clasped around them to help stop my shaking.

After a few minutes Graham said, "Feeling better now?"

I shook my head.

"Still a little green?" His expression was sober, but I saw the deepening smile-creases in the corners of his eyes. He wasn't taking this seriously.

"I could have been killed." My mouth tasted dry and acrid. It was difficult to speak.

"Surely not." His eyes still creased. "A frightening experience, I know, but—a fence?"

I knew I should be thankful for his calm ministrations, his unruffled concern. He was trying to be heartening, but instead his amusement irritated me. I was not at all feeling better. Rivers of sweat ran down my spine. At the same time I felt clammy and cold. My stomach quivered with fright. The gentle, faraway sounds of summer, which should have soothed me, were instead refrains of those I'd heard last night while waiting to hear the overdue sounds of Ross's car leaving Hamehollow.

Had he been doing something to my car in those minutes? My frequent meetings with Ross since we'd met flashed through my mind; the connection between us of my father and his uncle; a stone found, then found again along with something more, something to trouble Ben Gowan.

"My brakes didn't work. I couldn't stop. What if the fence hadn't been there? What if a stone wall had been there instead? What if I'd been near a cliff?"

"Now, Isabel...," he began.

"I could have been. How could he be sure I wouldn't?"

"He?" Graham didn't look amused any longer. "Who?"

"I don't know who," I conceded, after a pause. "Or why. But I think someone may be trying to kill me."

Nine

Why then, alas,
Do I put up that womanly defense,
To say I have done no harm?
—MACBETH, ACT IV, SCENE ii

By the time we arrived at the Digerness police station my trembling had subsided, but as Graham parked his car, glancing at me with questioning concern, doubts began to nag at me. I had certainly suffered unpleasant—even disturbing—happenings. I cataloged them: a witch's warning; my room disrupted; my drawings taken; a collision in the street; and now this, a car crash with little consequence. Each one with a plausible, innocent explanation. Could I convince the police that something sinister had happened? Had I totally convinced myself?

Without Graham I might not have gone through with it.

Without Graham I might not even have found the police station. It looked like a house, like all of the other houses on the street. A low stone wall surrounded it, and an iron gate led through to the garden. It sat at the end of the street. The wall rounded the corner, and there stood another gate through to another garden. Petunias and marigolds bordered paths to the house. But the path around the corner led to a door where there hung a blue sign saying *Police.*

I hesitated, uncertain, before pushing open the gate, and Graham politely reached around to open it for me. I had been committed.

Inside seemed more official. We came into a square room nearly filled by an old wooden desk and a modern swivel chair, a row of metal filing cabinets against the wall behind them, and three straight-backed chairs lined up on a side wall. A uniformed policeman looked up from some papers as we entered. He stood and reached out a hand to Graham.

"Graham. Good to see you. What can I do for you?"

Graham pressed me forward. "Isabel, this is Police Constable MacFee." And to the policeman he said, "Miss Garth is an American visitor. She has something she needs to speak with you about."

Constable MacFee studied my face for a second. "MacFee," he reintroduced himself. "Sit down, Miss Garth." He pulled over one of the straight chairs and held it for me. Graham sat along the wall, leaning forward on the edge of his seat, his elbows on his knees.

MacFee leaned back in his chair, looked from me to Graham and back to me, and lifted pale yellow eyebrows that matched his crew-cut hair. "What seems to be the trouble?"

"I've just had an accident. My car." I took a deep breath. I looked over at Graham, who looked back expressionless. Was I sure? Or had I been more disposed to alarm than I supposed by Thora and her divination? I made my voice firm. "I think someone may be trying to kill me."

MacFee bounced up straight, his fingers hitting against the desktop edge with a small thump. "That is a very serious allegation." After a pause he said, "This accident. When? Where? Apparently you were not hurt?"

"No. But only because—my brakes failed—had it happened somewhere else..."

"Where did it happen?"

"Coming back from St. Margaret's Hope. Just a little while ago. Half an hour? A tractor pulled out in front of me, and I couldn't slow, couldn't stop."

He got up half out of his chair. "The driver, where is he?"

"He didn't know it happened, he just went on. I didn't hit him. I hit a fence, instead."

"And your car?"

For the first time Graham spoke. "Not too badly damaged, I think, and still there, on the Millbrae Road. One of Davey Duncan's hire-cars. They'll have to do body work, I expect, the left bumper and a headlamp. And the brakes, of course, whatever went wrong there. Some dents and scratches, too—there was barbed wire." His face took on that mildly amused look he'd had at the car.

"Whatever went wrong with the brakes is what someone did to them," I snapped.

Constable MacFee frowned at the phone on his desk. "Excuse me." He pushed himself up and went through a door behind him. I stared down at my hands in my lap, hands that were beginning to shake again. Neither Graham nor I spoke. We could hear through the not-quite-closed door the bass drone of MacFee's voice, a short silence, then his voice again.

When he came back he said, "Now," with an air of getting on with things. He sat with his hands still on the arms of his chair, his elbows sticking out, as though his position was temporary. "You say someone tampered with your brakes so that you would have this accident."

"Yes. Well, not this one, exactly. No one could have known, could they? But whoever it was knew I'd drive the car all sorts of places, and would know I'd need the brakes. Just where..."

"An inefficient way to kill someone," he commented softly, almost to himself.

"Yes, I suppose it is. But it could happen. I could have smashed into the tractor. I could have swerved into the other lane and had a head-on collision. I could have killed someone else." A policeman should have known these things, how dangerous the loss of brakes could be, how easy it would be to kill, or be killed. "I could have gone into the sea somewhere. Or...," I thought of the rocky, winding descent from Hamehollow. The accident could have been there. It might have been intended that it be there.

My voice wavered. "Maybe someone didn't care if I died. Maybe someone just wanted to hurt me."

Belatedly, because he'd just thought of it, or because I was beginning to look as unsteady as I felt, Constable MacFee said, "Though you weren't hurt, you must be shaken. Perhaps you would like some water, or tea?" He sounded sympathetic, but when I shook my head he turned, businesslike again, to Graham. "You were a witness?"

"Not to much of it. I saw the car hit the fence post. I didn't know then it was Isabel, I just stopped to help if I could."

"And the tractor? Did you see this tractor?"

Graham shook his head. "Must have been out of sight by then. The road's a bit of up and down right there. But I didn't look. I didn't know then what had happened."

"Isabel you called her." He was still speaking to Graham. "You knew Miss Garth before the incident?"

"We met on Friday," I told him myself. "Ross MacDonald introduced us."

"Ah." After a short silence MacFee said, "Perhaps now would be a good time for you to explain why anyone should be wanting to kill you."

I spread out my hands, then quickly clasped them again.

"That's just it. I don't know. Ross MacDonald has been . . . I arrived on Thursday. I met Thora, who claims to be a witch."

MacFee nodded. He knew who I meant.

"She warned me of danger, told me to go home. I didn't believe her, of course.

"Then I met Ross, at the inn. Furrowend. Meggie Denison, who runs it, introduced us. And I've seen Ross for one reason or another every day, sometimes several times a day, since then. Wherever I go . . . it's almost as though he's been arranging events so we'd meet. And I've had two accidents."

"Two!" said MacFee and Graham together.

"Someone ran into me."

"Into your car?" asked MacFee.

"On foot. Near the harbor. Someone dashed out and ran into me. Pushed me."

"Pushed you."

"I'm sure of it. I felt the hands on my back. I fell into the street. No cars were coming, so I only hurt my knees in the fall."

"Can you give me a description?"

I shook my head. "I didn't see whoever it was. Two women were near, they saw it all, but—"

"And who were they?"

"I don't know that, either, but they disagreed about who they saw. A boy, they thought. A black hat or black hair, or red."

"A boy?" said MacFee. "Or boyish? Red hair? Thora?"

"I thought so, possibly. But why? And would she do this to my car?"

He spread his hands, calling all of my assertions into question. "Would Ross?" he asked, and then, "And when?"

"Last night, at Hamehollow."

MacFee interrupted. "Hamehollow? Didn't you have injured knees? An odd place to go. Rather a climb, wouldn't you say?"

"A few scrapes." I'd said those words to Ross. "Meggie gave me a walking stick. And it's steep, but not far. My father used to spend time there, and I wanted to see it."

"Your father?"

"Callum Garth. He lived here long ago."

MacFee shook his head. "And Ross MacDonald went with you?"

"He came up later. He'd called for me at the inn. Meggie told him where I was."

MacFee said nothing, only waited.

"We talked for a while. He left. The thing is, I listened for his car to start. It took too long."

MacFee frowned.

"He should have started it right away, but he didn't, not for several minutes at least. Plenty of time for him to be damaging my brakes."

"You waited for him to leave before you left?"

"Yes."

"Why didn't you leave together?"

I looked at Graham, then away again. "We were both angry. He . . . he'd kissed me, and I pushed him away. He lost his temper, and left."

"Rude behavior, to be sure," MacFee said, "but it doesn't mean he was doing harm."

"He was angry. He shoved me, and ran off down the hill. But he didn't start his car and drive away, the normal thing to do. What was he doing? The very next day my brakes failed. And why has he been following me around? Besides—" There was something else, too, something small niggling in the back of my mind.

The phone rang, and MacFee answered it there at his desk. "Aye," he said into it. He listened, said "Aye" a few more times, and hung up.

"That was Davey Duncan," he said. "Your car will take a day or so to repair. He'll not do body work, but the brakes and the headlamp, those he'll do, and he'll deliver it to the inn as soon as possible. He'd give you another, but he hasn't one. Will that do you?"

"Yes, I suppose—but what about . . ."

"The brakes? Aye, there was a cut in the brake line. Not a large one, mind. As to when it happened, well, it could have been last night. Or even earlier. It sometimes takes a day or two for the fluid to drain away." He held up his hand before I could say anything. "You were at Hamehollow. The track is very rough there, is it not? Large rocks, and sharp with it, some of them. It could just as easily have been one of those as, say, a knife. An unfortunate accident, but there you are. An accident."

"But, James," broke in Graham, "you will talk to Ross, won't you?"

"Aye, right now, I think, we'll get to the bottom of this." He pulled the telephone toward him.

"Hello, Mrs. MacDonald. James MacFee here. I'm sorry to interrupt your tea, but I must speak to Ross." A short silence, then, "Ah, Ross. MacFee. I need to see you at the police house right away. Could you manage that?" He listened. "I can't say on the telephone, but we've a puzzle here I'm hoping you'll help us to solve. Good. We'll see you in a few minutes, then."

He offered tea again, and after I refused, Graham did the same. We didn't speak while we waited. Constable MacFee leaned back in his chair, his eyes closed, and tapped a pencil lightly on the edge of his desk. Graham stood at the window, staring out. I sat with my trembling hands in my lap and tried to capture an elusive thought.

Ross strode into the room, then spotted me and Graham and came to a halt.

"Hello," he said, his inflection making it an exclamation rather than a greeting. His eyes flicked warily around the room. "What's going on?"

"Sit down, Ross, and join us," said MacFee.

Ross sat in the chair next to Graham, pulling it away to put an empty space between them.

MacFee said, "Miss Garth has had an accident."

"Isabel!" Ross was out of his chair. "What happened? Were you hurt?"

"Oh, sit down, Ross," Graham muttered.

MacFee waved Ross back down. "I've asked you to come in because Miss Garth suspects you may have had something to do with it."

"Me?" He regarded MacFee, then me, his eyes questioning. "I don't even know what happened. What are you talking about?"

"Tell us about last night," said MacFee.

"Is that when it happened?" He turned to me. "Something happened on the way home, is that it? Did you fall? Oh, Lord, it was my fault. I'm sorry."

"I didn't fall, Ross. I had an automobile accident. And not last night, today."

"Today?" He looked baffled, then he grinned. "You Americans. I've heard you didn't take to driving here very well."

I remembered that first evening, the men from the garage watching me drive off so badly after Ross had left me there. Could they have laughed with him about it?

Ross turned his grin to MacFee. "Wrong side of the road, was it?"

MacFee went on soberly, as though Ross hadn't spoken. "Miss Garth thinks you may have interfered with her brakes last night, causing them to fail today."

"Now wait a minute!" Ross jumped up, an angry, fuming scowl on his face.

I said, "What were you doing for so long? When you left you didn't start your car when you should have."

"And that means I was fiddling your brakes? You should know

what I was doing. You'd got me all ... I was trying to regain my composure."

When I'd uttered the first words of my accusation, my misgivings had begun. Since Ross had entered the room, they had magnified. Now, though, I knew he lied. Our closeness at Hamehollow hadn't even quickened his pulse. I jumped up, too, my hands clenched into fists at my sides.

But MacFee broke in calmly, "You've seen quite a bit of Miss Garth the few days she's been in Digerness."

Ross pretended to think about this. "Yes, I suppose we have run into each other a bit."

"It's been more than that, Ross," I insisted.

"And perhaps not accidentally," suggested MacFee.

"Well ..." Ross slanted his gaze at me from under heavy lashes and said to MacFee, "All right, I suppose I did arrange our meeting a few times. So what? I wanted to see her."

"Why?" I asked.

"You know perfectly well why. Because I find you attractive. Very attractive."

"What about Meggie Denison?" asked Graham.

"Meggie's a lovely girl, but, well, that's just it. She's a girl. Naught but a wee lass. Besides, we'd been quarreling. And that's when Isabel—Miss Garth—came into the inn. I couldn't help it. I fell for her."

I snorted. "I don't believe a word of it."

"Don't you, though?" He gave me a slow, sleepy smile. "You believed it at Hamehollow, didn't you? And you didn't seem to mind a bit." His smile broadened, and somehow turned into a leer.

My cheeks burned, and I sank back into my chair. It was true. I had believed it, and responded to it. But only for a moment. And I certainly didn't believe it now.

"And before that, there was Friday," Ross continued.

"Friday? At the cottage? Or later, when I picked you up? Your car had broken down. You were stranded in the rain. Should I have left you there? I wish I had."

"You went to dinner with me. Who knows what would have happened if he hadn't shown up?" He jerked his head in Graham's direction. "But he did, so the next day you came calling at my house. Shall I complain you've been pursuing me?"

"I went to see your mother, to make a condolence call," I said, then stopped. I remembered Ross entering his mother's spotless room, his arm around her when we spoke of his uncle, and the thought that had been eluding me came clear.

"You didn't ask me, did you? You asked how I knew Thora, but you never asked how I knew your mother, or your uncle, Ben. Because you already knew. How did you know? And why?"

I didn't know how this could matter, except that he must have known, and shouldn't have.

Graham, Police Constable MacFee, and I all stared at Ross, waiting.

"Oh, all right," he finally said. "I suppose I'm just going to have to tell you the truth."

Ten

Thou com'st to use thy tongue; thy story quickly!
—MACBETH, ACT V, SCENE V

But he didn't tell the truth just yet.

He walked over to a map that covered a large part of the wall behind the desk and stood in front of it, his back to us. Ross affected to study it silently, the shape of the coastline, the pattern of roads, the dense cluster of building symbols around a crescent-shaped bay that represented Digerness and the lands wide around it.

The longer he delayed his story, the more it intrigued me. I waited impatiently, MacFee, Graham, and I all silent ourselves, for him to begin. It was several minutes before Ross said over his shoulder, "Sinclair must leave. This is none of his affair."

I expected Graham to protest. He had been involved, both in my rescue and in the accusations and excuses that followed. He must have been curious. But he nodded, agreeing. "He's right. This is between the three of you." He stood, crossed the room, and was out the door in one swift, fluid move.

I felt a momentary stab of indignation that he seemed so uninterested, so eager to be gone, but immediately forgot him in anticipation of Ross's truth.

In the closed room a hush returned. Ross faced us now, head bowed, and said nothing. I saw his lips move as if in unvoiced rehearsal, but still he did not speak. Several more minutes passed before he lifted his head and finally and simply said, "My uncle found a buried treasure."

The words caught me by surprise, and I swallowed back a gasp that had risen in my throat. I didn't want to make a sound, to move, to do anything that might interrupt his story, hardly yet begun.

But MacFee, beside me, said easily, "Aye?"

Ross came back to us and sank into his chair, letting our expectations build again before he continued, his face serious, his voice close to a whisper.

"He found a Viking hoard. A fancy box, all decorated with carvings, bone or ivory, and framed with silver. Not grand," he mimed a shape in the air with his hands, forming a square, fat book, or a deep cigar box, "but filled with gold and silver, jewelry and little carved things. I never saw them clearly. He never emptied everything out, or at least not in front of me. He seldom even opened it. He kept it in his room, and every evening he'd bring it into the parlor and just sit and stare at it. He liked the past, was always reading history books and going round to the ancient sites."

He lifted his chin, fixing me with his gaze. His face was still grave, but a gratified smile pulled at the corners of his mouth and reflected itself in his eyes. "He always envied me a little for my burnt mound. Aye, some would say 'twas his. I found it on his land, after all. But its glory belonged to me for finding it."

Then the near-smile faded, first from his eyes, then from his mouth, as the sense of his story came back to him.

MacFee and I waited without prompting while he found his place once again in his narrative.

"I suppose he was imagining who had owned the treasure, wondering why they'd buried it. This went on for many weeks. Then he told us, my mother and me, that he was giving it up to the authorities. Imagine, to have our treasure end up in a museum in Edinburgh. God knows what it was worth. Fine for rich folk, giving it away, but for us—we're just poor farmers."

MacFee grunted, and Ross hesitated, then replied to what MacFee had left unsaid.

"Aye, there's reimbursement, perhaps, but how much? And when? After forever in the courts. I wanted him to sell it. Plenty of people will pay a fortune for old things of any kind, no questions asked. With ancient gold and jewels we'd be rich." Ross stared down at his hands, open and empty. "He refused, of course, said it was his to do with as he wished."

"The law, Ross—" said MacFee, and stopped suddenly, as though deciding to let the tale continue and discuss the law later.

Ross went on as though he hadn't been interrupted. "My uncle became quite angry with me, wouldn't speak to me for days.

"He was angry with my mother, too. She wanted him to put the box back, to re-bury it where he found it. She's deeply religious, a faithful churchgoer, but she's superstitious with it. I suppose a few folk are like that, still partly believing the old stories about trolls and goblins guarding treasures, and she was sure if he didn't restore it some terrible vengeance would befall him."

"Hogboy," I whispered. I was immediately sorry, afraid he would think I was making fun, but he nodded gravely. He looked suddenly old, his cheeks sunken, blue shadows under his eyes.

"My mother was right after all. He had a cough he couldn't seem to get rid of, and eventually it got worse, seemed to turn into pneumonia. He went all the way to Edinburgh to see the doctors there. Lung cancer, they said. They gave him some treatments that just seemed to make him feel worse. He didn't want that. He made them stop. Came home to die in his own bed, with my mother to care for him as she always had. And he got better for a while, and we thought then that the doctors had been wrong. Or I thought that. My mother, she was convinced her prayers it was accomplished it. Either way, we both thought he was cured. We started in on him again about his find, each of us with a different plan, each of us for a different end."

Ross clasped his hands between his knees, his head down between hunched shoulders, as though all the air had seeped out of him. He spoke quietly then, as if he were talking to himself. "He knew he was dying, and there we were, fighting over this—thing. Then one day, after the two of us had been on and on at him about it, he slammed out of the house, the box with him. He was gone for hours, and when he came home he was exhausted and sick. And he didn't have the box. He never told us what he'd done with it. And we never asked. We were afraid to."

He raised his head, and I saw in his eyes the regrets, so like my own, that make up the worst part of grief. I looked away.

Ross said, "It seemed my mother had her way. He gave back the treasure. But too late."

He shook his head sadly, then more forcefully, bringing himself back from the past, back from the sensitive creature he'd momentarily become. "He wrote to you soon after he found the treasure."

So that was it. The letters. I hadn't imagined either Ross's attentions to me or that false air, that something amiss, surrounding them.

He continued, his tone accusing. "And then again a second time, at least, after he'd taken the treasure away. I know. I saw the letters—or the envelopes, at least. I even posted one of them for him. At the time I thought nothing of it.

"My mother nursed him. I took over running the farm. He liked to pretend he was still in charge. He still told me what to do. I let him, but I did what I wanted. I had to. After a while he didn't even know what season it was. I gave my mother a rest, sat with him when I could, and talked to him. Or listened to him rather, talk about the past. About your mother."

"My mother!" I had never truly felt the loss of my mother, because she had never really been gone from me. I'd been too young to remember much of her, but in part because of my father's memories, shared with me so often as to almost become memories of my own, she had always been with me, representing unconditional love. Like the laughing woman in the photograph that sat beside my bed, she was eternal and constant, and perfect. Now he was bringing her into this.

"My mother has been dead for thirty years."

"Your father brought her here once, did you know?"

"It was before I was born, or you."

"Aye. But my uncle fell in love with your mother. He was in love with her still when he died." Ross straightened a little, and his voice held an angry challenge. "He hid the treasure from us, his own family. He loved your mother. And he wrote letters to you."

"I'm not his daughter, if that's what you're thinking."

"No. He'd have said. But maybe he wished you were. He told you, didn't he? Told you where he'd hid the Viking box."

"No."

This made some sense, at least. In his driving need he'd imagined a reason for my presence, far from the simple reality. "He told me nothing," I lied. He'd told me so little, in that letter to my father. "He never mentioned anything about himself. I didn't even know of your existence, or your mother's. Ben Gowan wrote me as a friend, because his friend, my father, had died. To give me comfort."

"And to give you my inheritance."

"No," I repeated.

Ross seemed to sag, to give up his argument, as if he knew how absurd it was, how inconceivable that his uncle would keep from his beloved family, angry though he was with them, what he would give to a near stranger.

MacFee's calm, slow voice broke in. "Would ownership be yours, Ross?" asked MacFee.

"Or my mother's, you mean?" Ross sounded happy to be diverted. "Does it matter? But yes, it would. What money he had he left to her, but he left everything else to me. Providing I support my mother, allow her to live at Pentwater for as long as she wishes. Which means always," he added bitterly. "I can never leave, because she'll never leave. She's lived at the farm most all her life, all the happy times of her life. It's all she knows, all she wants. Yet I must sell it. If I must keep the farm and hire someone else to keep it going, I cannot afford to leave."

"But this place," I said, meaning Digerness and Orkney, "why would you want to leave?"

"Do you think I fancy being a farmer all my life?" Ross glowered at me. "Or living forever in this far-off, backward land? I want to go to Edinburgh, or London even. And I need money to do that. Money I could get from the treasure."

"No more, Ross," said MacFee. "Even with it lost again I'll have to inform the Heritage Society, the authorities. They'll investigate. And should you find it, you'll inform me."

Ross stood, and drew himself up. The shadows and hollows had disappeared from his face. This was the old Ross, sure and arrogant. "Would I not?" he said, but his look, and his next words, said otherwise. "No matter what happens, I'll do what I can. The treasure is mine, and I want it."

"And I'll do what I must," said MacFee. "If I find there's been criminal activity . . ." He let the threat hang in the air.

Ross shrugged, and made a tentative move toward the door. But I still had questions. "What made you decide I knew about the treasure? You said you'd known about the letters, and thought nothing of them. What made you change your mind?"

He made an impatient face, annoyed at my slow understanding. "You came to Digerness."

"But I didn't come to find a treasure."

He gave a short, sharp laugh, disbelieving, but he went on without further argument.

"Meggie recognized your name when you wrote for a reservation at the inn. Of course she knows about it, 'tis her future, too. I'd told her everything. She told me you were coming."

So he had been waiting for me after all, waiting with Meggie that first day at the inn. Their worry, their quarrel, had begun when I failed to arrive, and Meggie's triumph when finally I did.

"And you did come," Ross said. "That's when I knew for certain that you knew, that you were after it, too. Why else would you come here?"

If he expected a reply he didn't wait for it. He paused only long enough for a breath before continuing. "You knew something, for certain. You kept hanging about the cottage, where he'd found it."

Found it under the wall, I wondered? Had the stone my father found, a stone in his wall, marked the site? Was that why Ben Gowan had written to my father as he had, *I must have your advice?*

Aloud, I laughed at Ross's words. "Hanging about? Twice. And I told you—my father lived there as a boy."

"Be that as it may, I thought if I followed you about, sooner or later you'd lead me to it. And I thought if I . . ." he looked beyond me, into the corners of the room, searching for the right word, and finding it, looked back defiantly into my eyes, ". . . I thought if I wooed you I'd have good reason to be with you all the time."

"So that's why . . . at Hamehollow . . . you thought it might be hidden there." I didn't want to talk to him about Hamehollow, but he might have been counting on that, counting on my not questioning. It was true I'd been a fool, but he'd been deceitful, and he still hadn't fully explained.

"How did you know I'd go there?" I was sure I knew the answer, but I wanted him to say it, while another mystery unraveled itself in my mind.

"Meggie. She always knew where you were going. If you hadn't offered, she'd have sent you there. She's the one guided you, encouraged you, isn't she? A logical place to hide a cursed treasure, don't you agree? Hallowed ground? I'd looked there before, the first place I'd tried, and found nothing. I wanted you to go there, to eliminate that possibility, at least. If it was there, if I got close to it, surely you'd reveal it somehow in your manner."

"But you knew your uncle hadn't told me of it in his letters, didn't you? You knew that from the beginning. Because of Meggie."

His transparent half-smile told me I was right, and I continued.

"She searched my luggage, didn't she, my first day here, while you drove me to Duncan's Garage. And she found the letters, and read them, and knew they said nothing of a treasure."

"Not in those letters, the ones you brought, and left for her to find."

Arguing with him was useless. "And my father's notebooks, did she read those, too?"

He gave me a doubtful look. "I know nothing of notebooks."

Why should he know of them? Possibly Meggie had skimmed through them, pronounced them irrelevant, or in any event too long, and gone on to my drawings.

"My drawings?" I asked.

Ross lifted his shoulders. "I'll see you get them back. I don't know why she took them. They were of the wall, though, and Hamehollow. Significant places. I'd wished to see them, without much hope of their revealing anything. What could they show?

But you'd bothered to draw them, those tumble-down rocks, instead of pretty scenes. And Meggie tries to please..."

"How could she have done this?"

"Please don't be angry with Meggie," Ross said, his supplicant expression almost persuading me to forgive them both. "She was never happy about any of it, and that especially. She only did what I asked. She just wanted to help me get what was mine. She meant you no harm."

"Harm, Ross?" asked MacFee, reminding us why we were here, bringing us back to the beginning.

Ross looked surprised, then shook his head emphatically. "No, believe me, I never tried to harm Isabel. This accident, it really was an accident." He asked me, "Why would I want to hurt you? I wanted you healthy, exploring, digging even. I wanted you to lead me to the treasure."

But it was neither that simple nor that innocent. I had over-reacted, suspecting Ross of attempted murder, accusing him as I had, but not completely without cause. He may not have tried to kill me, but he'd been deceitful at the least, and it had taken my accusation to force him to admit that much. I'd seen his charm disintegrate, to be replaced by selfish arrogance and an explosive temper. I wanted to hold on to my anger, to the suspicions Ross's glib story almost dismissed. It was too easy to blame myself for being gullible, or to forgive him because I understood the pain in his eyes. I needed to get away from him. I wanted to walk, to jostle the pieces of his story into an imaginable order, to let the incessant Orkney wind blow the clouds from my mind. I didn't yet believe Ross, though he had explained away everything.

Or almost everything. I thought of Thora, of what I knew she'd done. "What about Thora? What part did she play?"

"Thora?" He looked puzzled. "What do you mean? She's not *my* friend. Why should you imagine she had any part in this?"

His puzzlement looked genuine. Perhaps he was telling the truth about this much, at least.

"Oh, all right. Never mind," I said. No doubt her role was as I'd thought, her own drama, orchestrated to her own design, nothing to do with the Viking hoard.

"Had anything more happened?" put in MacFee. "Involving Thora? I'll find those witnesses, and I'll speak to Thora concerning the attack on you. If she's done something else, you must tell me."

"Nothing. She gave me a warning of danger, and tried to make it come true. I didn't believe her. Naturally. Or believe in her. In her witchcraft, I mean. I still don't. I just thought if Ross had involved her ... but no, Thora's done nothing."

Eleven

Present fears
Are less than horrible imaginings.
—MACBETH, ACT I, SCENE iii

G raham had waited for me outside. I saw him around the corner as I came out, leaning against his car, his brown hair gleaming like copper, lit by a lone crepuscular ray of the sun. By the time I reached the gate in the garden wall he was there, opening it for me.

"Isabel. There you are. Good. I'll take you home."

"You shouldn't have waited," I said. I tried to smile, but my face felt set in an expression of anxiety, and I had to add, "You've been so kind already, but I don't think I can bear to be shut in the car." Glimpses of the sea sparkled between the houses down the hill, and the beginning of the seawall was just visible. I thought I could pick out the roof of the inn from the others at the bottom. "I need to walk, and it's not all that far to the inn, is it?"

I intended to go alone, but Graham was not so easily dismissed. He came with me, in a long, roundabout route that helped to slow my churning thoughts. I didn't know if I should be relieved that events had been so easily explained, or angry that I'd been manipulated so. Or even if, on reflection, that I should believe any of it.

Graham didn't talk, and didn't seem to expect me to. If he was curious about what had happened or what had been said, he asked no questions, but simply walked silently beside me.

We passed O'Hara's. A young couple came out the door, and noise and music rippled out with them. When Graham asked, "Hungry?" I was surprised to discover I was.

We bought ham sandwiches and walked down the hill to eat them on the seawall, tossing bits of bread to the squabbling gulls. A man mending fishing nets on the stern of his boat lifted his grizzled head from his work to simply nod in response to our waves. On the horizon, a line of silver separated the sea from the sky. We spoke hardly at all.

Only later, after we'd crossed the road to the inn, did he ask, "Are you feeling better now?" And when I smiled my assent he bent and lightly kissed my lips, then turned and walked away.

Had he meant the kiss for my comfort? It only added to my bewilderment.

The inn, too, was lively with people. The Digerness Festival was tomorrow, but people were beginning to celebrate tonight. The noise here was more refined, the laughter more subdued, than at O'Hara's, but the dining tables, normally laid ready for breakfast by this hour, were still filled with people lingering over coffee and drinks.

Meggie came through the door from the dining room. She smiled broadly at me, calling out, "Hello," as she crossed the lobby.

Seeing her, I felt a surge of anger, but it drained away as quickly as it came. I had no energy left for anger at Meggie. Besides, what would I say? I could tell Ross hadn't told her yet that he'd confessed, both to his own deception and to hers. And after all he'd done, her sins seemed small. Might I not have done the same not long ago for Allan, to keep him near me, to keep his love? Perhaps. Rather than feeling angry at Meggie, I might do better to feel pity for both of us.

"I'm glad I saw you," Meggie said, open and friendly. "Someone's left a package here for you."

She ducked down behind the desk, bringing up what looked like a book in a sea-blue bag from Spindrift. My name was scrawled across the bag in thick black letters.

I turned the bag over, looking for something more. "Who is it from, do you know?"

Meggie shook her head. "It just appeared on the desk. It could have been left by anyone, people have been in and out all evening. There've been more than usual tonight. Tomorrow is the Festival. We've all of us been so busy preparing, running here and there. I'll ask, but I think no one would have noticed." She put her palms in the air and shrugged. "Perhaps there's a card inside. Sorry."

One of the staff appeared at the dining room doors, beckoning frantically to Meggie to come help, perhaps with difficult diners or a problem in the kitchen, and Meggie rushed off, leaving me with my unexpected bounty.

In my room I looked for a card, and when I found none, for an inscription on the title page. There was only the book itself, the *Orkneyinga Saga*, with a bookmark dangling a gold tassel from its pages. The bookmark looked familiar. I pulled it out. It was a broad, white arrow of fine, crisp cloth embroidered in gold with an image of the Orkney Dragon, the edges rolled and overcast with gold threads that joined at the tip, then twisted down to the tassel. I had seen bookmarks like it for sale in Spindrift, handmade by Thora.

The gift could have been ordered by telephone, and delivered by the craft shop. But not ordered by Graham, though he'd recommended the book. He knew I'd already read it, and might still own a copy. And not by Ross, who also knew, had he been paying attention. Besides, a thoughtful gesture, without reward for himself, seemed not his style. Johanna and Andrew, eager to share the lore of Orkney, might have sent the book, but they wouldn't have included one of Thora's bookmarks.

But what did it matter who sent it? The book was what I needed now to forget the afternoon's catastrophes, to erase from my mind the jumbled images of unimaginable treasures and troubled, dead faces. The *Saga* could put me to sleep tonight, as it had years ago when my father insisted I read it.

I'd never been able to follow much past the mythical Nor and Gor, the Genesislike recounting of the many generations, the confusion of battles and continual divisions of kingdoms. I couldn't keep the characters straight, though as a child I'd loved their names. For years the outgrown stuffed toys on my bedroom shelves were named for the most outlandish among them. I'm sure I was the only girl in my school with a teddy bear named Thorfinn Skull-Splitter, and a stuffed rabbit named Erik Bloody-Axe. But tonight the tale itself was perfect, something ancient and seemingly unreal to soothe me, to bore me, to lull me into sleep.

I read about Harald Fair-Hair who, annoyed with the Vikings who staged their raids from the Orkney Islands, conquered and subjugated them. A Norseman named Sigurd became their first earl, and the Orkney Vikings became farmers.

But their raids continued. I remembered the prayer of the early monks on their small islands, places they'd once believed secure, protected by the sea: *From the fury of the Northmen, good Lord, deliver us.* Those raids, which had struck terror into holy hearts, were spoken of offhandedly in the *Saga*—a spring trip and a fall trip. Between planting crops and reaping, after harvest and before the icy winter rains, those sometime Orkney farmers once again became marauding Vikings.

Instead of growing heavy-lidded, I found my interest quickening, my eyes opening. The story still had an artificial structure: two warring brothers seeking to control the Islands, one eventually overcoming the other, and a kind of peace prevailing until his death. When his two sons succeeded him the cycle began again, jealousy and rivalry leading to wars, to deadly trickery, to terrible revenge.

Familiar names appeared. Earl Thorfinn, grandson of Malcolm II, King of Scots, was an Orkney Viking, raised for a time, I knew, with another of King Malcolm's grandsons, his cousin, Macbeth. Both true, the *Saga* and Shakespeare's *Macbeth,* and both fiction as well.

It was getting late. Through my window the sky still shone bright, but I could see town lights flickering on, and a green buoy light blinking out in the lucent water. I began to skim through the book, reading here and there, of an enchanted raven talisman, of a treacherous drink-fest, of celebrations ending in fatal fire. I read the poems. These brutal warriors celebrated not only their glories but their bloody battles, their killing fires, in a verse that combined realism with a singing symbolism, creating a bleak, fearsome beauty. Everything seemed black and red: black ravens of death, burnt-black decks and halls and houses, red flames, and always red, red blood.

Christianity came, at sword-point to some. Converted Vikings embraced their new faith fervently, as they embraced all else, with an enthusiasm that produced saints and miracles. But the old ways did not altogether die.

The *Saga* was filled with cruelty, greed, death, and treachery. But it was also filled with loyalty, bravery, and beauty.

The combinations of style, of myth and history, of pragmatism and poetry, of the kinships, gave the *Saga* a powerful Old Testament mood. Some of the early parts may have been myth, yet the reality of it was all around me—in old houses and churches throughout the Islands, in the runes scratched on the ancient stones of Maes

Howe, in Viking graves, in St. Magnus Cathedral, built to honor the Viking saint whose bones still rested there.

And in Ben Gowan's treasure.

Despite this reminder of the intrigue I'd found around me, intrigue now only possibly explained away, despite tales of sorcery and women named Thora, the *Saga* was finally having a soporific effect. Names repeated themselves. Events flowed into events. The inevitable cycle continued.

I dozed, and woke again in a tangle of sheets, the book face down on the floor. I picked it up. It had fallen open to a story underlined in black, like the writing on the bag it came in. Had the bookmark marked this page? If I'd opened to it at first and not looked instead at the bookmark, would I have found it then?

Harald and Paul were brothers. Each ruled one half of the Islands. Bitter rivals, they still strived for peace. They shared Christmas one year at Harald's home. Their mother, Helga, and her sister, Frakokk, had sewn a white linen garment, embroidered with gold. Harald admired it, and when they told him it was for Paul he seized it in a jealous rage. The women tore at their hair and cried for him not to put it on, but he would not listen. He put on the bewitched shirt. He sickened. A few days later Harald died.

All of the long twilight had gone from the sky. The few hours of summer darkness had begun. I closed the book around the bookmark and set it carefully on the nightstand beside my bed. The gold tassel, marking Earl Harald's story, spread itself over the painted wood.

The text here held no real terrors. There was no danger to anyone except to a man long dead. These events happened long ago and in an unreal time. Harald and Paul once lived, and Harald had died so Paul could rule, but he had not died of magic.

Yet these women, Helga and Frakokk, had worked their magic in fiber, in thread, as Thora did. Had their gold thread outlined an Orkney Dragon on the robe, as it did on Thora's bookmark?

The bookmark, the underlined passages—they were undoubtedly another warning from Thora, for in the margin, in those same black letters, was scrawled, *Beware! Danger may come from unexpected sources!*

This had to have come from Thora. I'd believed Ross earlier, when he said that she was not involved in his treasure search. Now I thought he'd lied. Thora's actions had to have some purpose, to be more than the theatrics of a self-styled witch. And I would find out what.

Constable MacFee had said to come to him again if I was bothered by anything. What would he say about this new menace, as real and threatening to me as it would seem vague and imaginary to him?

I got out of bed and wrapped my bathrobe around me.

Meggie had locked up the inn for the night. She was squaring the guest book and telephone neatly on the desk in the dim glow of the night-lights. She looked up, surprised, when I came down the stairs.

"Was Thora here tonight?" I asked without explanation.

"I don't know," Meggie said doubtfully. "She may have been." Her brow wrinkled in thought, then smoothed again in an easy certainty. "Aye, now I think of it I did see her. Was it she who left you the present, then?"

I nodded. Meggie's certainty probably was based more on a desire to please than an actual recollection, but I didn't really need her word. I knew. "Will you be here in the morning?"

"Aye, I'll be about quite early. Is there something you'll be wanting?"

"Perhaps. I'll see you then. Good night." I turned away, and climbed back up the stairs to my room.

I finally slept, and dreamed of Thora weaving linen spells with gold thread.

Twelve

If you can look into the seeds of time,
And say which grain will grow and which will not,
Speak then to me...
        —MACBETH, ACT I, SCENE iii

A s I came downstairs in the bright light of early morning I saw Meggie. I saw her hesitate and, pretending not to see me, march toward the dining room in affected haste.

I called out, and hurried to catch her at the door. "I had an accident with my car yesterday."

Meggie knew by now. Ross would have called her late last night. He'd have told her about my accident, my accusations, and his confession. As if in confirmation, Meggie nibbled on her lower lip, her eyes brimmed with tears, and she said, "I'm so sorry, Isabel. I really didn't mean—"

I didn't let her finish. I didn't want an apology. It would only nurture that wellspring of sympathy, that recognition of our oneness. Besides, I was telling her this because I had a plot of my own.

"Duncan's have my car," I said. "It won't be fixed until this afternoon at the earliest, they said, and they don't have another to give me. But I need a car this morning. Not for long, just for an hour or so."

Starting out the door with Meggie's keys, I eased my conscience by reminding myself that I hadn't really asked her for the loan of her car. Meggie had been eager to offer it to me.

It was a perfect day for a festival. The early morning air was warm, the sun already high in the cloudless sky. Across from the inn, in the flagstone square beside the Harbor Office, workers fought with the wind to string colored lights and pennants over the festival stage they'd constructed the day before. I watched the struggle for a few minutes before driving past and up the hill, to the road to Ben Gowan's farm.

I wasn't sure where Thora's farm was, only its general direction. I couldn't ask Meggie. She seemed truly sorry, but how could I know what relationships existed, what machinations worked beneath the surface of this pastoral peace? Better to drive a way, and perhaps ask at a croft somewhere, than to let Meggie know where I was going.

Just past my father's cottage I turned to the right, away from Pentwater. This was the way I'd seen the green car go, the one I'd been sure was Thora's, that day at the cottage with Ross.

Not far down the road a grassy track opened between two fields. A stack of grayed lobster creels leaned in an artistic disorder against a sign that said Skailsetter Farm. If this was not Thora's farm, surely the people there could tell me where she lived.

At the end of the drive a small cluster of stone buildings squatted in the sun. A dark green Beetle was parked on a square of gravel to one side of a house with a green painted door. I had no doubt. This was Thora's farm.

A huddle of long-fleeced sheep stared at me from behind a wire mesh fence that stretched between two of the buildings. As I got out of the car they crowded back, not taking their alarmed, wide-apart eyes from me. They pushed close again, on quick, dainty feet, when I started for the farmhouse. Smiling despite my mood, I continued to watch them over my shoulder as I passed. And as I did, I noticed that a door stood open in the smallest of the buildings. Forgoing the green door of the house, I headed to that one, instead.

The door opened directly into the one-room building. Two bulky looms filled much of the space. Nooks and shelves lined the walls, holding cones of threads, and yarns in an almost unimaginable variety of color. A deep blue weaving was still on one of the looms, most of its length wrapped thickly around the beam. Sunlight from a side window streamed through the cream-colored warp, casting a thinly barred shadow on the plank floor.

A cluttered worktable separated a small space at the back of the room from the rest. Beyond it I could see Thora and her mirror image moving together, partners performing a slow, turning dance in perfect symmetry.

Thora didn't see me at once. She continued to turn, to study her own reflection in the old-fashioned floor mirror, examining her costume from every angle.

She wore a long kilt, reaching almost to her ankles, fashioned from a tartan I doubted any clan would claim. The weave was of fiery pinks and oranges, and a deep ruby red, and through it, as through Earl Harald's fatal robe, was shot a thread of gold. The colors would have run together into a dizzying chaos except that an occasional stripe of pale, cool green offered rest and comfort to the eye.

Thora wore a plain white blouse above the kilt, and over that draped a long kilt sash in the same outrageous weave. It came up from around her waist and looped around her right shoulder before crossing again behind her to hang over her left, where it was clasped just above her breast with a thick round brooch.

Thora must have caught a glimpse of me standing in the doorway. Or did she feel my presence with those special senses she claimed to possess? She whirled around. She'd drawn her hair up into a loose bunch of curls at the top of her head, with brassy, corkscrew tendrils escaping to frame her face. She looked modern and smart, even beautiful, and not at all like the gawky blue-jeaned adolescent she had seemed on the pier. I could see now the Thora who must have attracted Ivor Denison.

"What are you doing here?"

Her tone was hostile. Had Ivor, despite his demand that I say nothing, even to her, let on to her that I'd seen them together? Just for a second I was taken aback.

But I had come for a confrontation, and I would have one. At least now there seemed no need for awkward beginnings, for explanations. I pulled the *Saga* from my pocket, and held it out. "You sent me this, I think."

"Not I." Thora shook her head, her voice still harsh. "Why should I send you a book?"

"Not just a book. This book. *The Orkneyinga Saga.* Someone left it for me at the inn. With this bookmark, linen and gold. One of yours. I've seen them at Spindrift."

Thora glanced at it, then away again with a dismissive shrug. "They sell them there."

"Whoever left the book left the bookmark in this place." I offered the opened book to her, but she ignored it.

"And this part has been marked as well," I continued, "and underlined so I'd be sure not to miss it. It's the story of the death of Earl Harald. I'm sure you know it."

Thora gave a little laugh. "Of course I know it. 'Tis a part of my history, that I learned as a wee bairn. But the book isn't mine. I didn't mark it, and I didn't give it to you."

"It was meant to frighten me." I waited for a response, but Thora simply stood, looking insolently at me.

"You're trying to warn me away, aren't you? Why? Even here,

in the book, someone—you, I'm certain—wrote a warning, *danger*. As you warned me in the beginning. And accidents, I'm sure you know, have been happening to me."

This time Thora shook her head. "I know nothing of that."

"You do," I insisted. "You pushed me into the street." And my car. Constable MacFee believed it really was an accident, but could she have done that?

"I've done naught—" she began.

We were getting nowhere, me accusing and Thora denying.

"Even if you've done nothing, you know something." I put the book on the table, holding it open to that place with a prodding finger, and leaned over toward her. "If you didn't give me this, tell me who did. And why. You can, because you're a witch, or so you say. Go on, then, prove it. Tell me what's going on."

Thora pulled herself erect and looked down her long nose at me. "I'll tell you that you know nothing of witches, nor of witchcraft. You think it is abracadabra, and silly people forming covens and performing black magic. Or spea-wives making kine barren and turning milk to vinegar. I *am* a witch, but not the sort you ken. I have magic you cannot understand. I hear songs you cannot hear. You hear the wind and the sea, and I hear them also. Yet I hear music of the stones, too, and of the very earth itself." She came around the table in long, strong strides, and stood close in front of me. She brought her face near, almost touching mine, and said with firm authority, "I don't make magic, I absorb it."

She turned away and busied herself with the clutter on the table, then turned back to me brandishing a pair of scissors in front of her.

A momentary, irrational fear seized me, and my hands shot up protectively over my breast, but Thora brushed past me to the blue weaving and began to cut it from the loom. "You'll have heard of our Festival?" she asked, in a conversational voice.

"Of course." The abrupt change, in subject and in tone, startled me into meek assent.

"They'll be giving a bouquet to our lady Member of Parliament this morning, with speeches and so forth, and handshakes all round, but 'twas me caused them to go away. Me!" She jabbed both forefingers to her chest. She still held the scissors with finger and thumb poked through the handles, and the point, wagging unheeded, scraped her, and left a bright red bead of blood on the tip of her chin.

Despite the confusion of pronouns I knew what Thora was talking about. She claimed for herself responsibility for warding off the threat of the local nuclear-waste site.

" 'Twas me and the magic I brought from the earth, and the plundered magic I gave back to it. Magic that gave back the power for the earth's refusal, and for that I've been given a gift from the dead."

Her words took on a new measure, the Norse rhythm of the Islands exalted into a hypnotizing song. "That magic you deride, 'tis nothing more than the past. And 'tis nothing less. Past gods and past cultures, with all of their great powers, not gone with death and time but locked into the earth with them. And I use those powers, through my sheep and with my looms. My sheep feed from the blessed earth and give me wool to spin. I spin, too, the clouds, leaving in the bits of blue sky that cling to them, and the sunrise and the sunset. And when I weave, I weave the waters below, the greens and blues and the deep cold grays, and the blacks of the midnight storms. Primrose and sea-pinks and oysterplants grow from my loom, and the mosses and lichens that blanket the beds of the graveyards, and the gray stones themselves. I weave dreams and memories, and the past and the present together. I weave the souls of the heavens and the earth."

She picked up an end of her sash and held it out to me, as if in illustration. "Sometimes I use the magic for myself, or weave it into other people's lives. But I return it, too, return it to the earth, with my prayers, my incantations, my rituals, even with my sheep. I call to the oreads, raise them from their death trances, and conjure them here so they may dance with me, to protect my sacred places, to keep them from destruction."

I had a sharp, sickening vision of a sheep, one of those whose innocent faces had greeted me this morning, but with its bloody throat gaping open, stretched on a rude stone altar.

"Oreads?" I asked. I didn't know what the word meant, and didn't want to know. But I had to say something, do something, to stop this inundating flood of words and images.

Thora didn't answer. She'd begun knotting together the warp ends of the weaving into a fringe, but now she dropped that and came over to me, again standing close, bending a little so that our eyes were level. "Who are you, that you fancy yourself so important? Do you think that I care about you? That I would waste my time with you?"

Thora's zealot's eyes bore into mine, and I dropped my own to her brooch. The brooch stared back at me with several large-eyed faces. Strange figures, men or animals, made a torturous pattern in the gold, their heads attached to sinuous bodies, their limbs twining and reaching, hands and prehensile feet grasping everything they touched—the rim of the brooch, each other, even their own necks. I could feel Thora's breath on my face, and imagined that I felt, too, the many breaths of the tiny creatures.

Thora's passion, her sure arrogance, unnerved me, and my old doubts came rushing back.

Thora, sensing triumph, pressed closer. "I've done nothing to you but to tell you the truth." Her voice came on at me as if from far away, in that mesmerizing Norse sing-song. "I've felt a danger for you from the first, and I've tried to give you warning. Blame me if you like, for whatever you like, but I've done no wrong. I've put no spells upon you. I've conjured no evil spirits."

Thora lifted her head, like an animal sniffing the air, and turned away. "I feel danger still around you, but it doesn't come from me. Listen to me. Go home."

She was finished. She had dismissed me, forgotten me. She went back to her mirror and began again the critical examination of her garment, her magical weave of the Orkney sunset. The ruby red now seemed to me Viking fire, or blood. The cool green line no longer summoned rest, but a cold, drowning sea.

Despite the open door the room felt airless. My temples throbbed. Sweat trickled down my spine. The colors of the spools on the wall began to pulse, then spin, then vibrate back and forth, exchanging places with each other in a reeling kaleidoscope. I ran outside.

I leaned against the car and pressed my forehead to the cool metal, staring at its black paint to crowd out the colors behind my eyes.

I'd forgotten even to confront her with having shoved me. I accepted defeat. I was sure now I'd never know Thora's purpose, or even that she did, in fact, have one.

I noticed then that I still held the *Saga*. I held it with my finger marking a page, the place, I was certain without looking, that told of Harald's death. I didn't remember removing it from the table. I thought at first I didn't want to see it again. Then, with a small resurgence of pride, I remembered that this was my history, too. I had always thought of it only as my father's, had valued it for his sake. Even my coming here had been for him. But though I had not been born here, had not been shaped by its seas and its stones and its winds, I, too, belonged to Orkney.

I straightened, my spirit and body stronger, but it was several minutes before I felt able to get into the car, and when I started the engine my hands still trembled. I turned the car with a spray of gravel and sped without caution back to the inn.

I'd been gone just over an hour. The workmen had finished.

The stage, clothed in banners and buntings, waited for the celebration. Inside the inn Meggie and her staff hustled between tables, serving breakfasts. I was thankful not to have to stop. I tossed Meggie's car keys onto the desk and ran up the stairs to my room, and back to bed.

Thirteen

...this night I'll spend
'Unto a dismal and a fatal end.
—MACBETH, ACT III, SCENE V

A loud wail jolted me from sleep. Startled and disoriented, I could only lie in bed until it smoothed itself, accompanied by a tattoo of drums, into a bagpipe melody. The Digerness Festival had begun.

I watched from my window. Crowds had already gathered to listen to the speeches. Three men conferred on the stage, while another tapped the microphone. Its screeches joined the music of the Highland band, piping and drumming in the street surrounding the stage.

The musicians wore matching black jackets and boat-shaped bonnets dangling long black streamers down their backs. Their kilts were in a variety of plaids, familiar, traditional plaids, some of which I might even be able to name. Unlike Thora's plaid.

By the time I got downstairs it was already afternoon, but the speeches were still going on.

Ivor Denison sat with others on the stage. Across the street

Meggie and her mother had come out of the inn, and stood in the doorway watching. Called to the dais, Ivor was recognized for his work as a trustee for the Pier Arts Center—in Stromness, but benefiting all of Orkney—and for his generous gift of time and effort as cochairman of the Digerness Festival Committee. As he responded, his eyes behind their round lenses raked the crowd. But I had already looked, and not found Thora.

It was Ivor himself who then presented a framed award to a woman with a politician's smile, an award for her success in keeping the nuclear-waste site away from Digerness. The award Thora thought she herself deserved, for what she and her magic had done. No wonder Thora was not here.

At the end of the ceremony the leader of the pipe band, waiting nearby, raised his long, silver-headed staff. The drums rolled, the bagpipes played again. At their moorings in the harbor the boats bobbed on the gentle swell as if swaying in time with the music.

Then, with a flourish of drumsticks and a swirl of kilts, the band began a slow march down the street. Like the children of Hamlin, the crowd followed, and me with them, down the shore and up the Breckan Road. The tea shop there had set its chairs and tables out on the pavement and, along with the usual hot tea, sold lemonade. A long line of children waited before an ice-cream van, wriggling impatiently, jiggling their coins in their pockets and fists. Above it all the sky rode still a cloudless blue, the sun shone intently, and the sea might have been the Mediterranean.

A group of men sat on a bench beneath the Spindrift sign, leaning toward each other, their heads together in gossip. I recognized John Rousay's bobbled tam, and then Uncle John himself, in rapt discussion with his friends. If he was here it meant his wife would be inside. Johanna had said she and Andrew would be here, too, and would introduce me to Nan today.

And Thora? Had she come here, instead of watching Ivor? Her

weavings were sold at Spindrift, and her daring costume would be the perfect display of her unique skills. I didn't look forward to meeting her again today, but I wouldn't let the prospect keep me away.

Even so, I might have wavered if John hadn't looked up as I hesitated before the shop door, and lifted his hand to me in a shy, sketchy wave. He smiled, too, and my faltering spirit revived. I hadn't realized until that moment how much I had been looking forward to seeing this normal, uncomplicated family again.

The little shop bustled with people. I looked for Thora, and found Bea MacDonald instead, her shining black head bent over a table while she carefully refolded a rumpled pile of sweaters.

I saw Andrew, too, looking small beside a tall, blond couple who were alternating their attention between Andrew and a lively, colorful crazy-quilt hanging high on the wall.

"Isabel!" Johanna shouldered her way through the shoppers. She threw her arms around me like an old friend. "I'm so glad you've found us. Come. Meet Nan. We've been telling her all about you, and it's time you met."

Nan, tall and straight, with a silver braid curled to the crown of her head, stood behind a table near where customers browsed through felted mittens and hats. She took my hand between both of her own. "Do tell me you're having fun on your holiday and not being bothered anymore by our fey creatures."

I saw Bea MacDonald look up sharply, and Nan said quickly, "Bea, this is Isabel Garth, from America. I'm afraid Thora frightened her a bit with talk of witchcraft when she arrived. We're hoping she's enjoying her stay with us nonetheless."

"Oh, but we've met before," I said. "Mrs. MacDonald gave me a wonderful tea."

Bea nodded, as though acknowledging a truth. "I'm happy to see you're up and about," she said. "You've had no ill effects from your fall, then?"

My fall? Ross must have told her about my collision in the street.

"Fall?" Nan and Johanna said together.

"A stumble, really," I reassured them. "I scraped my knees a bit, that's all."

"It hadn't anything to do with...?" Johanna let the rest of the question hang.

No need to concern her with Thora or the rest. I shook my head, and she changed the subject with obvious relief.

"Isn't it wonderful, all the people here today? Andrew and I weren't supposed to be working, only Nan, but when we came in with her we were conscripted. Thora was supposed to be here but—a headache, wasn't it, Bea?"

"Aye, she telephoned me this morning. A migraine, she said. She gets them terrible sometimes."

Andrew interrupted, leading over the couple he'd been talking to. He grinned his hello at me, then said to Nan, "They'd like to buy your quilt, Nana, and take it home with them to Sweden. Shall I get it down?"

Nan flushed with pleasure. "Fetch Uncle John. Ask him if he'll come in to help you."

"But, Nana," Andrew complained, "I can do it myself. I climb up ladders and ropes and bars all the time at school."

"At school 'tis different."

"No, just the same. The same as helping with the scenery when we do our dramas. I can do it, Nana, truly." He tilted his head down so that he had to look up at her through his long dark lashes. A well-practiced look, and charm enough for any grandmother.

"Well..." Nan's pause was long enough to allow Johanna to add an objection, and when Johanna said nothing, Nan sighed heavily. "If you'll be very careful, then."

We watched silently while Andrew positioned the ladder,

climbed easily up, took down the quilt without hesitation, and climbed back down.

For the first time I saw Bea MacDonald smile. " 'Twas right to let the wee one do it," she said. "Aye, these lads can climb about like mountain goats."

Perhaps her mood was lightened by the brisk sales and the festive atmosphere. It seemed infectious. I did some shopping of my own. Impulsively, I bought a woolen stole in numberless hues of blue and green, like the land and sea and the sky above Digerness gathered together on Thora's loom. I decided I should welcome her impressions of our shared heritage. Besides, what better souvenir of my time here than a wrap fashioned by a witch?

I bought a sweater, too, with lines of Viking runes knitted into it, runes that formed a pleasing pattern around the hem of the garment, but more than that, represented letters forming words, the words forming a phrase, and though I should have had enough of cryptic messages, I hoped that these symbols contained one.

"Can you read this?" I asked Bea as she folded the sweater into a square of tissue paper. "What does it say?"

Bea glared at me, and shook her head. "It says naught. 'Tis a mockery is what it is, and is asking for trouble."

"Oh, Bea," laughed Nan, her color and spirits high. "I think it's quite nice. And now I've sold my quilt, I'll buy something for myself, too. That weaving, Bea, I'll have it."

Nan said to me, "One of Thora's creations, based on an old traditional pattern called a summer-winter weave. Lovely, isn't that? She's done several rather like it, and I've long admired them."

The weaving combined deep blue and white in a thick, almost raised, geometric pattern repeated over its surface. On the other side the image and ground reversed themselves, giving the same pattern a wholly different feeling. It was very like the one I'd seen on the loom in Thora's studio that morning.

I felt a twinge of guilt, remembering the morning. Could I

have been the cause of Thora's headache? She hadn't seemed upset by my visit. Quite the opposite. It was she who'd dominated the meeting, and I who'd run away. Thora had gone back to her mirror as though nothing had happened.

But Thora had worked hard for this day, had believed that it was, in truth, in her honor. Now Thora lay in bed, while I enjoyed myself here amid the music and crowds and the magic of Thora's craft.

My morning's dizziness returned.

Johanna produced a chair from somewhere almost immediately. "Sit," she said, "you'll feel better. Nan will be off-duty soon. We'll all go for dinner." She lay a sympathetic hand on my shoulder. "This doesn't last, you know. A month, or two perhaps. Then your body will settle down."

How did she know? I put my hands to my cheeks. Did I already have that glow people talked about? Or did it simply take a mother herself to see?

When other co-op members arrived to take over for the evening and we were ready to leave, Nan said, "Bea, you've worked so hard today. Why don't you join us? We're dining at Furrowend."

"Oh, no," Bea shook her head. "I've Ross's tea to get."

"We'll run you home, then, shall we?"

But Bea shook her head again. "Thank you, but Ross will be collecting me soon. And after he's eaten I'll have him take me to see the lass. I'll take her some soup. I doubt that Thora has eaten all the day."

We left her there, waiting at the window for her son.

The air was still warm and fresh, and I began to feel better as we walked the busy street to the inn.

"Bea was the same with her brother as she is with Ross," Nan told me. "Devoted herself to him. He was older than she, and never married. She was like a wife, only more hardworking than many. She did everything in the house and garden, and more besides. She spins wool as well, for Thora and for many crafters in the village. She makes her own bit of money that way. Ben was good to her, too, of course. He'd taken her in. She was widowed, already middle-aged, with Ross just a wee bairn, so I suppose she felt obliged to him. Still," Nan sighed, "I hope I didn't hurt her feelings when I referred to Thora as fey. She's a bit fey herself, is our Bea.

"Or so some say. Folk knowledge, or even simple common sense, is sometimes mistaken for second sight. A few superstitions remain in parts of Orkney. None serious, you understand. The old beliefs make wonderful, romantic stories, and of course they're part of our heritage. We wouldn't want to forget them. Some people make too much of them just to make their lives more interesting. In Thora's case, her pose gives her comfort, I think, and a sense of power over her life."

We'd reached the inn, as bustling with people as the tea shop and Spindrift had been.

"As well we walked," said John, and waved an arm to the parking lot, where every space was filled, some cars hemmed in by others parked behind them.

I saw my own little red Renault returned there, its crumpled front fender marking it unmistakably. I would say nothing about my accident, and no more about the fall.

But the fall was the first thing Johanna wanted to know about once we had ordered our dinners. "Now, you must tell us how you happened to be given tea by Bea MacDonald. And your fall. It's no good saying it was only a stumble when Bea called it a fall."

"But I did stumble," I said, and began at the beginning to explain how I knew Bea MacDonald. "Ben Gowan was an old friend of my father's, ever since childhood. I called to tell him I'd arrived, and learned that he'd died. So I called on Bea. And later, in the village, I somehow tripped and fell."

"And no danger." Johanna smiled, relieved, and I smiled back.

Nan said, "Are you finding your way around, seeing all you want to see?"

"So far," I said, and I told them about my father's journals. "And I've found where he used to live. The MacDonalds own it now, and Ross took me around. Could you have known my father?" I asked both Nan and John.

Nan shook her head, but John leaned back in his chair, his eyes closed tight in thought. "Sorry, lass," he said finally. "I canna call him to mind. He'd have been a wee bit younger. No matter today, but 'twould have been a wide gap then. I'd no have noticed him, unless," he said, sliding a puckish grin toward Nan, "he had a bonny sister." His face grew sad, as though he'd failed me. "Fifty years and more have come and gone since."

"I'm happy you found his home, at least," Nan said.

"I've found most of the places he mentioned in his journals. There are only a few I haven't visited yet. Mostly, though, I want to wander now, to draw the landscape, and the flowers and birds. Some I know, but I wish I knew them better."

"Uncle John does," said Andrew. "He's a bird-watcher, he's head of their club. He knows all the birds. I know them, too. And the flowers. Uncle John taught me. And I can show them to you, thousands, when you visit us tomorrow."

Johanna opened her mouth to speak, and Andrew quickly added, "Uncle John and I can show you."

"Aye, that we can," said John, "with pleasure."

"And we'll show you Uncle John's tomb," said Andrew.

"His tomb! That must be the something special you promised," I said, and saw Andrew glance at John with a look like a shared secret sign.

"Aye," said John, "special indeed. A Stone Age grave. Not

grand like Maes Howe, nor even as complex as those some crofters have found. A peedie, simple grave, but exciting to discover all the same. A family plot, most likely, for the folk who inhabited and farmed our land all those centuries ago. Still, you'll see it only from afar. It stands too close to a crumbling cliff edge."

"Come early in the afternoon," Johanna said. "You can tramp to the cliffs with Uncle John and Andrew, if you've a mind to. Then you'll stay for a meal with us."

"Are you sure?" I demured, though I hoped they'd all agree. I wanted very much to see their birds and their tomb, and more to be with them for the day. "You'll want to rest tomorrow, not entertain."

"A birding walk will be a rest for John," Nan said. "And Andrew never needs to rest, it seems."

"And as for Nan and me," said Johanna, "we've already made a great pot of Scotch broth, more than enough. We won't have to cook at all. We'll have scones and stew, a simple farmhouse meal. You'll like that, won't you? And afterwards you'll entertain us with more tales of your holiday."

"You promised," Andrew said with finality.

"So you did," John concurred. "And while she won't be as fine a day tomorrow as today, we must go while the weather holds." He pulled a large round watch from his pocket. " 'Tis gone ten o'clock," he said. "If we're going home the night, we'd best go now. We've all a busy day tomorrow."

Nan yawned in response, and Andrew, trying hard not to, did the same.

As they gathered their belongings, Johanna mapped the way to the farm on the back of a Spindrift bag. "Until tomorrow, then," she said. "Shall we expect you at one o'clock? Sleep well."

But this was not the night for sleep. The inn, normally silent by this hour, still rang with the noise of the Festival. From outside came the sounds of more merriment, of people calling to each other, of bursts of laughter and loud conversation. Though the darkness had not yet come, the decorative lights had all been lit. The Highland band was gone. A rock band resounded in its place, its performers strutting upon the stage instead of marching in the streets. It jangled the village with a modern beat, no louder than the pipes and drums, but more strident, more insistent.

My head began to beat as well. I need a quiet place, I thought. How would the *simmer dim* look tonight from Hamehollow, with every light in the village shining, the strings of colored lights, the many mooring lights in the harbor?

I knew I wanted to go to Hamehollow again. It would be a kind of test, of my belief and my courage. Ross hadn't been totally convincing yesterday, and since my meeting with Thora I didn't know what I believed anymore. I would be vulnerable there, exposed and alone. But despite Thora's foreboding I knew I was not in danger. Alone was what I required, what I was certain I would be. Tonight I would not see Ross there, nor anyone else. Everyone else was here, making noise.

I was right, at least, about all the people. There were no cars where the road began to climb the hill, and none where I parked in the level, hard-packed space near the top. Since few people would walk all the way from Digerness, I knew, for now at least, I was alone here.

The evening had begun to cool, and as I climbed the rising wind brought the sweet smells of the clover and heather, still strong from the heat of the day. Clouds gathered in the distance, purple streaks edged with light. The low slanted sun spotlighted the ruin above. It sought out the gaps in the wall, caught the pinks and oranges of the wildflowers growing on the other side. Their colors showed through the breaks in the stonework like little pieces of sunset.

But no flowers grew there. I would have remembered their blaze of color, the picture they made. I would have made drawings of them. I was still a good way from the hilltop when it occurred to me that I was not seeing flowers at all. And with that thought came the dreadful realization of what I would find when I reached the ruin.

It couldn't be. But nothing seemed to make sense in this place right now, no more sense than this. I knew I was right. My breath came in quick, shallow gasps. My heartbeat echoed in my ears. I tried to run, but the ground slid under my feet, and I had to catch myself with my hands. I tore my eyes from the wall and what lay behind it, and concentrated instead on my feet, on the deliberate placing of one before the other, carefully, on the uneven ground.

Three gulls, squawking their complaints at my arrival, rose from their high gable perch and sailed off on angled wings. I stood, panting heavily. Some part of me didn't want to reach the top, too reluctant to find what I knew was there. If I didn't see it, it might not be true. But it was.

Too quickly, before I could fully prepare myself, I reached the wall.

I told myself it would be stupid to scream. Against the crying of the wind, no one would hear. And no one was close enough to hear. Still, a sound escaped me. A protest. An apology. I dropped to my knees beside the body.

Already there were flies, fat and torpid. I flailed at them, tears streaming down my face, cursing, as though the flies had done the killing. But my efforts had little effect. The flies rose idly, and hung, thick and clinging, just beyond my fingertips, then sank again to their odious task.

The body lay at the foot of a high span of wall. Her legs were curled up like a sleeping child's. One arm twisted beneath her, the other reached out in the direction opposite from her legs. Her face turned to the sky, held there by stones that seemed to cradle her head. Blood had flowed over the stones, seeped into the ground, and flattened the grass around them to a brown and sticky mat. Her open eyes stared at nothing, dull and lifeless, their faded color seeming no more than a clouded reflection of the blue of the sky. Her skin looked thick and waxy, her freckles dark, standing out sharply against the yellow pallor. There was a crust of blood in one nostril. A slender thread of it had trailed out, slanted across her upper lip onto her cheek, and disappeared beneath the curve of it. A thought came to me, sweetly sentimental, and I tried to push it aside, but I found myself repeating it like a mantra: *her thread of life*, I thought over and over, *unraveled*.

I brushed again at the flies. Their heavy bodies flashed with an obscene iridescence as they droned off just beyond my reach. Quickly, before they could re-settle, I drew one end of the brilliant tartan sash protectively over Thora's cold, dead face.

He is noble, wise, judicious, and best knows
The fits o' th' season.
—MACBETH, ACT IV SCENE ii

I did not kneel long beside Thora. Minutes, or mere seconds, made endless by despair. Still, sharp rocks dug into my stiffened knees. My hands, clasped tight before me as if I'd been praying, though I didn't remember that I had, had gone white and blood-less. My cheeks felt tight with dried tears.

I needed to leave, to tell someone. My mind urged flight, but my body, as in a nightmare, felt too heavy to move, too weighted to the earth by death. And some part of me wanted to stay, to hold watch, to keep vigil over Thora.

A dark bird winged overhead, trailing behind it a wavering lament. There'd been too many deaths. First my father's, then Ben Gowan's. And now Thora's.

Grief for Ben Gowan belonged to Bea and Ross MacDonald. Let them mourn him. I hadn't yet finished mourning my father. I hadn't yet forgiven myself for feeling unburdened when he died. But I was mourning him, and would miss him forever. Who would miss Thora? Who would remember her brief years, and weep because their brilliant promise had ended? Ivor Denison's owlish face appeared to me, lowering, disapproving, and quickly faded.

The grass rustled behind me. A rush of wind, a twilight creature? I whirled around, rising. I saw nothing around me but desolate, lifeless stone.

Why had she come here tonight? She'd stayed away from the Festival—to simply avoid seeing Ivor, or had she really had a headache? Had she had a ritual to perform here for herself, one to cure herself?

This was once a holy place. My eyes darted from one to the other of its murky, malevolent recesses. It had been a Viking church, Ross had said, before it became a house, before it became a ruin. Had it been one of Thora's ceremonial sites? I looked up at the crumbled wall, pictured her atop it in a healing dance, and felt an icy quiver across my shoulder blades.

My mind flew in swift illusions, trying to recapture Thora's day, to reinvent it, as if in doing so I could change the dreadful outcome.

But no matter how often I brought Thora safely into the village to sell her weavings, then sent her driving home in her dark green Beetle, home to her sheep, it always ended the same—here, like this. With death.

It was almost dark now. The broken walls I'd not long ago imagined as romantic and picturesque threw sinister black shadows across the scraggly ground, as if attempting to hide the sharp rock falls and outcrops lurking like concealed weapons. A dangerous place, Ross had called it. They should tear it all down, he'd said. Maybe now they would, when they learned how it had killed Thora.

Goosebumps crawled across my skin. I felt a sudden urgency to be gone. I ran, stumbling, back to my car.

I was surprised to see that the party in the village had not
ended, that the square by the Harbor office was still crowded with
revelers. Under the colored lights couples still danced. The young
still bounced and gyrated face-to-face, the old still shuffled cheek-
to-cheek. Festive people watched and laughed and talked together,
and overflowed into the streets.

My surprise was not because the hour was too late, the night
too dark, nor because the day already should be ended; but more
because the day now ending was not the same day as the one that
had begun. Life had changed, and this, too, should have changed.
I felt a brief, unreasonable anger. I wanted to shout at the people
my terrible knowledge, to see their faces change, their gaiety fade.
But how were they to know?

I threaded my way through the village. A policeman stood at
a corner talking with a mob of teenagers, and I almost stopped
my car right there, in the middle of the road. But the policeman,
too tall, too heavy, with black hair instead of yellow showing from
beneath his checker-banded cap, was not Constable MacFee, and
in my wretched state I wanted to talk only to Constable MacFee.
I drove on to the police station.

Most of the windows of the police house were dark. Music
and laughter from the Festival carried up through the night.
MacFee, too, might be down there, somewhere in the crowd where
I would never find him. But around the corner a light shown over
the door and poured out from one small window.

I pounded on the door and pushed it open. The police office
was empty, but I heard MacFee call, "Hold on, I'm coming," and
he entered through another door.

"Now what's so—" He looked at my face and said no more. He
reached out for my hand and led me into the room he'd just left.

The room was dark. The light that spilled in from the rest of the house showed a pair of high-backed chairs on either side of a fireplace. As MacFee put me into one, its wings massive and enveloping, I noticed that although he'd probably been in uniform, his white shirtsleeves were now rolled up, his collar gaped open and bare without a tie, and he wasn't wearing a jacket or shoes. He's off-duty, I thought, and I wondered stupidly if he would still talk to me.

"Jess," he called over his shoulder, and a round face appeared in the lighted doorway, then disappeared again.

MacFee bent over me, his hands on my shoulders. "What's happened? What's wrong?"

Surprisingly, since my legs had not yet stopped trembling, my voice sounded steady. "It's Thora. She's dead. At Hamehollow. She must have . . . she fell . . . I found her there."

"You're sure."

"Yes. Her head, it's——" The sight of that waxen face above the jagged rock and the blood-soaked ground came back to me. My throat constricted, and my voice gave out. I couldn't speak any longer unless the tears flowed with the words, and I already ached with crying.

I became aware of the woman moving silently in, setting a mug on the table beside my chair, and fading into the shadows of the room.

MacFee seemed to need no more from me. He spoke into the telephone as he shrugged into his jacket and pulled on Wellington boots. He kissed the air in the direction of his wife, and was gone.

Although the sun had shone all day, a fire must have lain ready in the fireplace, for as soon as Jess MacFee put a match to it, it flared into a smoky, earthy warmth. She pulled the other chair closer to mine and sat in it, but she didn't speak.

I took the heavy, homey mug in both hands and drank, letting the hot tea burn in my throat, and all the way down. It was good to feel something, anything besides that choking, aching sorrow.

After a time Mrs. MacFee began to speak softly. I heard her say something about her family home near Lairg, and about her small son and his even smaller sister, asleep a few rooms away. For the most part, though, I heard only her soft voice, and the ordinariness of the things she talked about. Soon death seemed unreal and far away.

It must have been hours before MacFee returned, bringing reality with him like a rush of icy air into the close, sheltered atmosphere of the room. He pulled off his jacket and boots with a great sigh that became a wide yawn.

Mrs. MacFee brought him a mug like mine, and he took her place in the chair next to me.

"Did you find...?" I asked.

"Aye, we found her. Everything's been taken care of."

We sat in silence for a while after this, while he drank his tea and studied my face as though it alone might tell him something. Eventually he put down his cup, placed his hands on his knees, and said, "Now. You've suffered a terrible shock, I know. But I must question you. I think you're up to it. First, tell me what you know of this."

"Nothing. I just...I found her...that's all."

MacFee said nothing. He closed his eyes and laid his head back, but his chair, a little smaller than mine, was too short for it. He raised his head again and looked wearily at me, waiting.

"She was supposed to work at Spindrift today," I said finally. "She didn't come. She had a headache. A migraine, Bea MacDonald said."

"And Hamehollow? How did you happen to go up there again?"

"I needed the quiet."

He nodded. Even in the closed house we could hear the thumping bass of the music rising from the harbor.

"You parked—where? The same place as before?"

"Yes. There isn't anyplace else, is there?"

"No, of course not. No other cars? Coming or going? You saw no one else?"

Did he think I wouldn't have said? Did he think I wouldn't have screamed for their help, wouldn't have dragged them with me back to Digerness, to him? I shook my head.

"And you were alone. You once thought you'd been assaulted at Hamehollow. You were not afraid to go back there by yourself?"

I could only shrug. "That first time—Ross explained all that. And I couldn't sleep. I had a headache."

"You had a migraine as well?"

"No. An ordinary headache. And now it's worse." Suddenly I felt exhausted, and I began to cry again, the tears flowing freely down my cheeks. "I'd like to go back to the inn now."

"Aye," said MacFee. "I'm sorry. You've had a frightful time. You're very tired. I'll take you back." He rose stiffly, with another long sigh.

"I have my car."

"Of course you do. But we'll leave it here till morning."

He said it decisively, as if it would do no good to argue. I had no strength for it at any rate, and was not sure I had the strength, either, to drive myself the short distance back to the inn. I followed him through the police office to the door.

He stopped and turned back to me. "You said before—let me remember—you said Thora had threatened you."

"She didn't threaten, she warned me."

"Tell me again. You knew her, how?"

"I met her on the pier the day I arrived. She was showing off, performing, pretending to be a witch—" That sounded mean-spirited, and I hadn't meant it to. I took a breath, and tried to make my voice sound calmer, kinder. "She said she felt danger for me."

Then, with a cold, dreadful stab in my stomach, I thought, Thora had sensed it all wrong, hadn't she? The danger that finally came was her own.

MacFee was asking, "Then, you allege, she attacked you. When you met her the next time, when you spoke, did she feel that danger again?"

I'd met her the next time at the inn, and she had all but ignored me. She hadn't even been aware of my presence when I saw her with Ivor at the Pier Gallery. She hadn't felt danger then. But I answered, "Yes."

Now he would ask me when this happened, and I'd have to tell him about all those times, and about the *Saga*, about that morning, and our argument. I couldn't. I couldn't make my mind form the words, or my voice say them. I couldn't change anything. I knew nothing to help MacFee understand her death. I was too tired. And even if I hadn't been, I couldn't talk about Thora anymore.

But he didn't ask. He drove me in silence to the inn, and took my arm as he escorted me to the door. He offered to take me all the way to my room, or to ring the night-bell for Meggie, but I convinced him I was fine now on my own.

So he left me at the front door. The darkness had already lifted from the deepest hour of night. I watched him walk back to his car. As he opened its door he looked up and said, "You won't leave Orkney without letting us know, will you?"

Give sorrow words. The grief that does not speak
Whispers the o'er-fraught heart, and bids it break.
—MACBETH, ACT IV, SCENE iii

Ach, the poor lass," said Uncle John.
I'd heard him say those words once before, when he drove us all to Digerness on the day I arrived—the day I'd met Thora. Then I'd been unsure if he was referring to me or to Thora. Now, hearing his words as I came into his house, I was sure he meant them for me.

Nan, on the other hand, said nothing. She folded me in an embrace as comforting for its aroma as for its warmth. She smelled soft and powdery, like the flowery talc I remembered wafting from the hugging mothers of my childhood friends. I was glad I'd come to Otterness Farm.

I'd almost not come. We'd arranged for my visit when the sky had been blue, when we thought Thora was safe at home in her bed. Now, on this gray, wet day, in the aftermath of disaster, the idea seemed at once too dismal and too festive.

But Johanna, on the telephone that morning, had disagreed.

"We've all heard. It's just too tragic. News like that goes round the island with the wind. And she was our neighbor. We're stunned, of course, and saddened," she said. "And you must feel especially horrid, finding her like that. And you've likely not slept. But you'll only feel worse if you shut yourself up in your room all day, won't you? The best thing for you is to be with friends. And we're the closest thing you've got here, aren't we?"

Johanna's sympathetic voice had become a little teasing at the end, but now grew serious again. "And to tell you the truth, we need you."

"Need me? Whatever for?"

"For Andrew. He's quite upset about Thora's death. Well, we all are, but—"

She didn't finish her thought, but began anew. "Andrew didn't truly know her all that well. The few times they came in contact she mostly ignored him. He was too much a child, too much beneath her, I suppose. But he was impressed by her. You could tell that, couldn't you? And this is the first time in his life he's been this close to death. He's at that age now to begin to think about it, to worry about me dying, or his dad, or—" Her voice broke.

"Yes," I said. I understood that Johanna worried, too. That she couldn't bring herself to name Nan or Uncle John when talking about death.

"Now it could be himself he's worried about as well," Johanna went on. "Thora was so young. Not that much older than Andrew, when you think of it. He won't discuss it with any of us. He's not said much at all, just moons about, silent, and we need to talk openly about it. It will help if you're here."

"But how? If he won't talk to you . . . I wouldn't know what to say. Besides, I'm upset myself. Most of the time I'm fine, but when I least expect it I begin to weep."

"So much the better. Sorry, what I meant was, it will be good for Andrew to see that you're upset, see that it's natural to cry. Or to laugh if you feel like it. And we won't even have to talk to him, to lecture him, that is. If you're here we can just say all the things we need to say, but to each other, don't you see?"

"My car..." I began, conceding. I didn't know if my car sat in the parking lot below or in front of the police station where I'd left it last night.

"Don't worry about your car. I'll come and fetch you. You won't want to cope with driving today, especially in the rain."

So I'd had no choice. And now that I was here, having been fetched by Johanna and an unnaturally silent Andrew, I already felt better.

We'd come into the house through an enclosed porch furnished with wicker chairs drawn up to a round pine table piled with magazines and paperback books. The deep window embrasures harbored treasures from walks—stones and shells and sea-bleached sticks and feathers. I thought of my father then, about his collections, and the collections my imagination had gathered in his boyhood bedroom, and wondered how much he'd been like Andrew.

I hung my rain jacket with the many others layered on hooks beside the door. Below them a clutter of boots, probably once in an orderly row, tipped over and heaped upon each other.

Inside, the house was tidy, but gave the impression that this was temporary, that the tidiness would soon disintegrate into the same snug, intriguing, lived-in disarray as on the porch.

I looked around the room, and saw Thora's weaving, the one Nan had bought at Spindrift, draped casually over an upright piano in the corner, the fringe spilling onto the keys. Only yesterday morning I'd seen one on Thora's loom... I couldn't go on with the thought, despite the purpose of my visit.

I dropped my gaze to the piano bench, covered with toppling stacks of music. I couldn't bear to look at Thora's creation. How could I talk about her? This plan of Johanna's wasn't going to work.

I sat awkwardly on the sofa, looking at the circle of concerned faces, and tried to think of some helpful way to begin.

It was Nan who finally broke the stillness, and began the flood. "You must have been frightened," she said simply.

I told them, then, more than I'd told MacFee. I told them about the *Saga*, about my visit to Thora's studio, about that last fateful trip to Hamehollow.

"I wish I hadn't gone to see her. It wouldn't have changed anything if I hadn't, but I think I wouldn't feel quite this bad."

"You wouldn't?" asked Andrew. Until now, he hadn't seemed to be listening. He looked directly at me for the first time since I'd begun. "Why?"

"Because we quarreled. I was angry with her."

"Because she frightened you?"

"Because she wouldn't tell me the truth."

Andrew nodded thoughtfully, was silent for a moment, then said, "Do you feel too sad to go to the cliffs with Uncle John and me, to see the birds? Come on," he said, suddenly animated, and pulled me to the porch, "I'll find some wellies for your feet."

The only boots not impossibly small proved too large, but I was grateful for them. The rain had diminished to a fine, warm mist, but the grass would be long and sodden. I pulled on a pair that came to my knees.

"You'll need a stick for the birds," said Andrew, handing me one similar to the walking stick that Meggie had loaned me. "The boxnies and pecky-ternies will swoop at our heads." He brandished his own, long and sturdy, and curved at the top like a shepherd's crook. "Hold it only a wee bit above your head, and they'll attack the stick instead of you."

An aging Border collie with a graying muzzle but darting, intelligent blue eyes waited for us just outside the door, as though he'd known we were coming. "This is Munro," said Andrew.

And the dog, staying close in front of John, led us through the farmyard, past a paddock where a short, stout pony stood, head down and her back to the wind.

"Who would have a pony here?" I asked, though I could guess. "Is it yours, Andrew? Do you ride it?"

"Aye. I used to ride her," Andrew said, a little regretfully.

At the sound of Andrew's voice the pony raised her head and regarded us through her long blond mane, then hung her head again, going back to her slumbers. Her coat was pale brown, and her tail swept the ground in the wind.

"You're both too old, lad," Uncle John reminded him.

Andrew nodded. "Aye. I've grown too tall." He smiled suddenly, as if he'd just forgotten to be sad. "So Nana and Uncle John bought me a new bicycle. They had it here for me when we came, as a surprise. I've one at home, you know, but this one is to stay here, to be waiting for me whenever I come."

He skipped ahead, his happiness enduring for the moment, and he led the way with Munro through the fields, opening and closing the gates for us. Nearby sheep kept watchful eyes on us, and a respectful distance from Munro.

Still faster than Andrew, the old dog slipped under the gates and leaped upon and over the stone fences, but stayed close, stopping occasionally to look back, to be sure we all followed.

A hawk flew over us, coursing low over the pasture, banking and turning on long, slim wings.

"A hen-harrier," Andrew told me uncertainly, glancing to Uncle John to see if he agreed.

"Aye, good lad," John said, bringing another smile to Andrew's face.

"They once were almost gone," Andrew said, "from here, at

least. But we brought them back." Andrew spoke with pride, as though he'd accomplished this feat himself.

After passing through the last gate, leaving the fields behind, we waded through untamed, uncropped growth, lifting our feet to avoid the grasping tangles, until we turned on to a wandering, uneven path, and walked in single file.

"This is a fowlers' path," said John. "Folk used to take the birds' eggs, or catch the birds themselves for food or oil. A dangerous task. This was the way they came to the cliffs, where they'd climb over the edges to the nests."

"I can climb—" Andrew began.

"No, lad," said John. "We'd sooner keep you than have some wee bird egg. No climbing."

The path rose steadily. It was well worn by the trodding feet that had made it, but no longer much used. It was threatened now, almost disappearing into the surrounding vegetation. We followed it up.

Soon I could hear the waves breaking, and the clamor of the birds, but I could see little but the path rising before us and the wild growth on either side. On the side toward the sea were flowers, and I longed to get closer to them, to study them, to be told their names. When I'd left the inn that morning I had, by habit, stuffed my pocket-sized sketchbook and my pencil into my jacket. I longed to make sketches of the flowers. But John would not allow it.

"We must keep to the path till we come to the right place," he cautioned. "The clifftops here are unsafe. We canna go near to the edge just yet."

So we continued to walk the path. We watched birds fly in from the sea, thin fish dangling from their overstuffed beaks like silver spaghetti, until, mysteriously, John stopped and said, "We'll go to the edge now."

To me it looked no different from any other place we'd passed, but John saw something I could not. We followed him across increasingly rough, rocky ground and approached the cliff edge. Munro circled us now, trotting around from one to the other, staying close, keeping us herded and safely away from the edge.

John pointed along the ragged coastline to the cliffs we'd avoided by staying on the fowlers' path. "You see why you must use care," he said.

He didn't need to say more. The cliff faces spoke for themselves. They rose up in uneven crags and ledges, eroded and undercut. Their grassy overhangs projected out from their shattered, concave sides high above the water, with nothing between their jutting green tops and the sea but emptiness. Emptiness save for the constant comings and goings of the birds.

Their noise was deafening, their numbers infinite. All kinds and sizes of birds soared and circled, plunged to the water, rose and landed, and took off again. Each cleft, each projecting stone that we could see, was occupied.

John pointed again, and led my gaze to a closer spot, halfway between us and this edge. The land rounded up to a gentle rise, and near the top of the rise I saw a gaping hole. At first I thought it was natural. Everywhere around us layers of rock pushed out of the ground at an angle, forming slanted walls and sometimes, where they fractured off, cavities. But the walls of this cavity dove straight down. The hole, despite long slabs that breached its length and reached above it, was roughly rectangular. The square, yellow-lichened stones that bordered it lay level with the ground.

"Your tomb," I whispered, and John and Andrew beamed.

"Years ago, before the storms made that place so perilous, I found it," John said. "A terrible storm had come, and tore away some sod. I was needing plainstone to repair a wall, and it was easy to get it here. But a hole appeared when I pried up a stone.

When I investigated, I could tell this was no ordinary hole. It proved to be a tomb. Wee and simple, but ancient."

He put an arm across Andrew's shoulder. "We've more to show you, just up here."

We walked close to the edge a few feet in the other direction, along a gently sloping rim where the cliff sides stepped out instead of in. We were close enough to see below us, where lazy waves broke against the small craggy shoals that pierced the surface of the water.

"Look," said Andrew. "Selkies!"

Two seals floated below, their large, sleek bodies plainly visible in the clear water. They swam at the foot of a broad pinnacle just before us. From where we'd stood near the tomb, this had seemed a point of land. Close up I saw that, except for a turf-covered rock bridge, it had been separated almost completely from the mainland. Eroded on all sides, it rose up from the sea, a column of stone shelved with birds.

"You've seen the Old Man of Hoy," said John. "One day, perhaps, this will be a sea-stack like that. But this one is different. Can you see it?"

I pictured the Old Man of Hoy towering over me on the *St. Ola*. This stack climbed not nearly so high, and here on land we were on a level with it; I could almost reach across to it. But there was another difference. I could see through the grasses, parted and laid flat by the wind, that the stones on its top were too regular, too ranked, too many, in fact, to be natural. I looked more carefully and could almost imagine that they composed one arc of a circular wall.

"'Twas once a hermitage," John said, "of a long-ago monk."

"Someone lived there? There's no room. How did they do it?"

"Those holy men in Britain at the time of the Vikings often built monasteries in treacherous, inaccessible places, places larger than this, and perhaps a wee bit more easily reached. We've a few of those around on the Islands. They were monasteries, religious communities. Some men, though, were simply hermits who preferred to live alone. They'd build solitary stone cells for themselves like this once was. Not much left to see, but not much to begin with. Little more than the walls and roof. A stark, severe life they lived, like some folk thought the way to please God."

He was holding Andrew's hand, and said, "Don't go too close, even here. Some think one reason the monks chose these places was their dangerous approach. Kept them safe, you see. Who'd go out there to kill a wee hermit, and not even have gold to show for it? Who'd risk that bridge at all, save a fool?"

He couldn't have seen Andrew's eyes widen at that, but I did.

"But the wonder is not in the past," John continued. "'Tis now. The hermitage proved safe for one monk, and is safe for the birds who live there now, as well. Leach's petrels, they're called. Wee birds, like swallows, dark with but a little white, and long forked tails. Rare birds. Or rare nests, at least. We've long seen the birds here, but knew of only one nesting site, elsewhere on the island. Till we found this one."

"Where is it?" I asked. I shaded my eyes to scan the hermitage remains and the sky, teeming with birds, around us. "I don't see nests, or small birds, either."

"Aye, not now, but come night, ach, that's a different tale. The wee ones are there now all right, but quiet. Making some noise, I ken, though we canna hear it. They live in rabbit burrows sometimes, or like here, in the holes and hollows made by the stones of the ruin. The grown ones, they're out to sea all day, fishing. They fly just above the water, barely stop to rest. The name, petrel, it comes from Peter, they say, Saint Peter, because the birds when they're fishing look like they're walking on the water. And the parents don't come back till night, when their enemies, the gulls, are sleeping, to bring the food to their chicks. And then, ach, doesn't the noise begin?"

Andrew danced around him saying, "Do it, Uncle John. Show her what it's like."

It was obvious that Andrew had seen and heard all this before, and loved it, and was eagerly awaiting John's performance for me.

John raised his head and closed his eyes, and produced a rattling, laughing cry that rang above the noise of the gulls and the nesting birds all around. Andrew laughed and clapped his hands, and John, still calling, began to bow and turn. He flapped his arms first fast, then slow, and bounced his knees, while he swooped and turned. His eyes were screwed tight, his cheeks sucked in, and through it all his brown knitted tam sat squarely on his head, the pom-pom bobbing in time with his large body.

He swooped one last time and was still. But only for a second. "And here's the wee ones," he said, and he began to purr and chirrup, a low rattled cry that raised in pitch and volume until it ended in a loud *whew.*

John sank to the ground, flushed and exhausted, while Andrew and I applauded his performance.

We were still applauding when I saw Andrew cast a worried glance at the hermitage. He hadn't looked in this way at the other dangerous places, at the crumbling cliffs, at the tomb about to plunge into the sea. Why at the hermitage? I wondered if Andrew had crossed that narrow bridge before. But he only looked, and turned away, and said nothing.

We walked farther along, following the still curving edges of the safer, sturdier cliffs. Andrew, only occasionally needing John's prompting, named the birds for me. White fulmars sat almost motionless among bunches of pink and white flowers that grew in soft mounds out of the sharp crannies. One of those birds ruffled its feathers and shifted, revealing a downy ball beneath it, with two tiny black eyes. I filled several pages with plump white birds brooding powder-puff chicks, while Andrew and John watched in fascination. Once home, I planned, I would do a drawing for each of them on fine paper, as a remembrance of this day.

Cramming the narrow ledges beneath the fulmars were tiers upon tiers of black and white guillemots and razorbills.

"And look over here," said Uncle John.

He insisted that Andrew and I inch to the edge of the precipice on our knees, so we could peer over it safely, into the rocky recesses below.

Four birds stood on a ledge. "Puffins," pronounced Andrew, and he grinned proudly, as though he had put them there himself, to show off just for me their giant red and orange bills. The puffins behaved as though they didn't see us, or as though their clownish colors had accustomed them to stares.

We walked back toward the tomb. Each time we stopped and looked down we saw the seals sweeping the water with their large flippers, moving with us around the headlands, watching us with huge eyes as we watched them.

From our safe distance we once more admired the tomb. A few days ago I'd been reluctant to enter Maes Howe. But when I had, its walls had not closed in on me, its air had not deserted me, its ghosts had not assailed me. So when I learned of this tomb I'd hoped to be allowed to crawl into it, to descend a little into the earth, possibly even to touch the ancient bones. But Maes Howe, when it was found, had contained none. Perhaps this small tomb, too, contained none. "Did you find bones?" I asked John.

"Aye, we did. Bones and skulls. Five thousand years old, they were. Archaeologists came from Edinburgh and dug some more, and took the bones away with them to study."

"Took them away?" I thought of my father, whom I'd so recently watched being placed ceremoniously in his grave, and of Thora, not yet buried, and never far out of my mind today. "It was a grave. Ancient, but still a grave. Someone buried those people. How could you let them be taken away?"

"The choice was no mine to make. Besides, there's no one left to care, is there?"

"Does that matter? When people are buried, they're expected to stay buried forever, not to be dug up for study."

"They'd no stay there forever in any event. Not many more storms will blow before the tomb itself will wash into the sea."

If I'd been told this the day before I'd have thought it a tragedy. Now I said, "That's better than ending up in a laboratory, isn't it? People are sometimes buried at sea, aren't they?"

I hadn't intended to criticize him, only those who'd emptied the grave. But I saw now I'd hurt his feelings. He stared inland, his eyes focused somewhere far away. Their blue was faded and clouded, and for the first time I saw him as an old man.

" 'Twas a long time ago, lass," he said quietly. "We didn't think like that in those days."

He waved his arm toward the vague gray distance. "I've a bit of fence to look to just there," he said. "Thora's fence. I'll go alone." He glanced at Andrew, who stood apart from us, intent on scratching Munro's ears. "No sense disturbing the lad," he said in a low voice, "reminding him. He's happy enough now." He walked away.

"I'm sorry," I began to apologize, "I didn't mean..."

What didn't I mean? I'd suggested he was wrong for finding the grave, for digging it and allowing it to be emptied, and now he was hurt and angry. And no wonder. I tried to run after him over the stony, spongy ground, but even with my long legs the oversized boots kept me lagging further and further behind. "Wait!"

He turned and shook his head kindly at me, "No, lass, I ken." He continued on, calling back over his shoulder, "I'll no be long. Thoo and the lad will stay where thoo are till I'm back."

Thoo. It was an affectionate pronoun, used to address children and small animals. My father had used it when he was feeling especially pleased with me. John now used it in speaking to Andrew and to me. I'd been forgiven.

Andrew appeared to have noticed nothing wrong between us in the first place. He stood with his back to me, hands in his pockets, looking out at the wheeling, screeching birds. "Such a grand spot here, isn't it?" he asked, with the proprietary air of a middle-aged laird.

"Grand," I answered. "Thank you for showing it to me."

"I'm not allowed to come here on my own." He turned and spoke directly to me.

"I'm not surprised. It could be dangerous, couldn't it?"

"I did, though, once." He came closer, speaking softly, so that I barely heard him above the raucous noises of the cliff. "Last summer. I was exploring. I wanted to find something important. On my own. A tomb, or a treasure." His confessional quiet took on a conspiratorial tone. "You won't tell, will you?"

"No, I won't tell. But you shouldn't have come. And you didn't find anything, either, did you? A good thing, too. It might have gone into the sea, and you with it."

I'd said it lightly, without thinking.

Andrew looked alarmed, then nodded agreement. But he still looked worried. There was something more.

I asked, "Did something happen to you then?"

He looked up at me with his round dark eyes. "It was Thora," he said. "She was there."

"There?"

"Out there. On the hermitage."

I looked across to the small near-island, the steeple of rock, then down to the sea breaking a long way below. "You didn't go there, too?" I asked, frightened for him even though it was long past.

When he shook his head I said, "But what was she doing out there?"

"Dancing. I suppose it was a dance she was doing, moving her arms about and swaying. She was singing, too, though it didn't sound much like singing. More like a funny humming, really. She sounded . . ." he screwed up his face in serious thought, searching for an apt comparison. "She sounded like bees in the heather."

The idea must have pleased him. A brief smile lit his eyes, then quickly disappeared. "I watched her. I couldn't help it. I tried not to, but I couldn't turn away." The youthful bloom of his cheeks turned bright red. He tucked his chin into his collar and muttered softly, "She was *naked*."

Performing her witchcraft. One of her prayers, her rituals. For her weaving, or for the land? I remembered vividly Thora's brief majesty, the intensity of her raving. I knew how Andrew felt. No wonder he had been spellbound.

"It's all right," I told him. "I understand."

"She didn't, though," he responded glumly. "She became quite angry when she saw me. She had no right. I never wanted to see her like that. And she didn't even know I had, not at first. She finished dancing, and she came back here. She didn't hesitate, or take care, or anything. She just stopped dancing, and ran across that little bridge without even looking, like it was nothing. I was so frightened. I was sure she would fall, I was waiting for her to, but all of a sudden she was here, standing in front of me, glaring at me. She didn't even pick up her clothes. She called me names, peeping Tom and worse. I didn't even know what some of them meant. She said I was a nasty little spy and I'd be sorry. But I told her I wasn't any of those, I just came here and couldn't help seeing her, and I really didn't want to. Then she laughed, really hard, and she almost hugged me, but I didn't want her to do that.

" 'Tell you what,' she said, and she picked up her clothes and finally started to put them on. 'We'll keep this our secret. You don't tell anyone you saw me here, and I won't tell anyone I saw you here. Your mam doesn't allow you to come here alone, does she? So we'll each keep mum, then, won't we?' That was a joke, you see, so it meant she wasn't mad anymore.

"She had a bag with her, and she got her scissors out of it, and she said, 'Give me your finger,' and I did, and she pricked it, and then did her own, and we held them together while she said some words." He held out his right forefinger, as though I might still be able to see the wound from which his blood had oozed to meet Thora's. "We made a blood pact that we would never tell."

He had told his story with barely a pause, as though he'd been rehearsing it in secret for a long time. He took a deep breath and blew it out with puffed cheeks before he said, "Now I've told you."

"It doesn't matter any longer."

"No."

He threw his head back and opened his mouth, as children do to catch rain, but I was sure he was collecting the mist on his face to disguise imminent tears. Beyond him, far off, I saw John approaching.

"I don't think it counted, anyway, telling me. She meant, don't tell your mother, or Nan, or Uncle John. I'm an outsider."

"I never meant to tell anyone at all, and I didn't, not till now. We had a blood pact. Besides, I couldn't anyway, could I? Not without getting myself in a jam." He shook his head. "But that's not it," he said. "The thing is," and he studied the toes of his wellies for a second before continuing in a small voice, "I didn't want to. The pact, I mean. I was scared. Scared of her. Angry with her, too. It was all her fault. She shouldn't have been here, either. I never said it out loud, but I said it to myself. I wished she'd fall."

I understood. It explained his fear, his anxious glances toward the hermitage. "She didn't fall here, Andrew."

"I didn't wish she'd fall here. I only wished she'd fall one day.

I forgot about it. I quit being angry, but I never took it back. It came true."

"No. Things happen, or they don't, for all sorts of reasons. But never for wishes. It doesn't matter what you wish. Even if you'd said it out loud, it wasn't your fault."

"You were sorry and you didn't even know her," Andrew said. "You cried for her."

"Yes."

"I didn't. What if I meant my wish? Even if I didn't make it happen, what if I'm not sorry that it did?"

A tear brimmed over and ran down his cheek. I reached out and wiped it away with a finger. "Was that for Thora?"

He looked up, surprised, and nodded.

"There, you see, you've cried, too. You're sorry after all."

If charnel houses and our graves must send
Those that we bury back, our monuments
Shall be the maws of kites.
—MACBETH, ACT III, SCENE iv

T he sky lifted as we walked back to the house. Faint light
seeped through dark clouds, giving a promise of sun somewhere beyond.

John raised a critical eye to it and shook his head. "Won't
last," he said, but as usual he didn't explain, leaving me to wonder
if it was the rain or the sun that wouldn't last, and if his knowing
this was based on a countryman's lore, or on some other sign that
I failed to recognize.

I didn't care if tomorrow we would have rain or sun. What
mattered was that the anxiety and tension between John and me
was gone, and that Andrew's confession had seemed to lighten his
heart. We filed back toward the house in a contented, companion-
able silence.

When we reached the pastures Andrew ran before us as he
had on the way out, opening and closing the gates. Munro, close

at our heels, herded us through and urged us toward home. This time, though, Andrew collected wildflowers.

"No rare flowers," he assured me, "just what are really weeds." I carried his stick for him, and daisies and yarrow and thistles filled his hands, but not yellow flag irises from the bog on the other side of one of the fences. At a gate he would clutch the flowers all together, to work it one-handed. Or almost. He balanced on one spindly leg while he used the other to help him, with amazing success, to maneuver the gate.

Andrew added to his prickly bouquet until we neared the farmhouse, discarding the blooms broken and strangled by his tight fist.

Once in the house, he broke the bunch in two, and with an elaborate bow offered out one in each hand to Johanna and Nan.

"How lovely," Johanna exclaimed. She sniffed recklessly at a giant prickly thistle and glanced at me over it. Her glance was questioning, and grateful.

Nan said, "We'll put them on the table, shall we, so we can enjoy them as we eat."

She handed Andrew a pottery jug. Its thick, imperfect rim told me it was handmade, probably bought at a years-past craft fair. "You've done so well to choose them. You'll be the proper one to arrange them, won't you?"

So both the bouquets, suitably praised, were given back to Andrew. He didn't so much arrange them as stuff them in as they were, as tight a fit as they'd been in his fist, and push and pull them into a rough kind of order. He set the jug with a clatter in the center of the round dining table, releasing a shower of raindrops and pollen onto the white cloth.

I saw Johanna's mouth open to scold and then close again. There would be no criticism today, nothing to destroy Andrew's fragile well-being. The wet, yellow ring lay around the pitcher throughout our meal, a golden symbol of the success of our outing.

During dinner, and after, we talked about the birds.

"You went to the hermitage, didn't you?" said Johanna. "Did you see our petrels?"

"You can't see them in the daytime," Andrew reminded her.

"Aye, of course. I'd forgotten. They did tell you about them, though?" she asked me. "Our rare nestlings?"

"Oh, yes. And we heard them," I said, "or at least, we heard and saw a wonderful impression of them."

"Aye." Nan laughed. "He's famous for his bird impressions, is John. Entertains at meetings and church socials and the like. And what about the tomb? Of course you saw John's tomb. What did you think of it? Isn't it marvelous?"

I glanced at John, hoping to find something in his expression, some hint of how I should reply. But before I could, a car sounded on the gravel outside.

Nan rose from the table, and said casually over her shoulder as she headed toward the door, "I hope you don't mind, but I've invited Graham Sinclair to join us for our coffee and sweet."

Graham? It surprised me at first. But of course they would know him, as they knew Bea and Ross MacDonald, and all of the other residents of their part of the island. Even those who, like Graham, lived halfway to Kirkwall.

"We'll have our coffee here, shall we?" Nan said brightly when she came back, leading Graham by the hand. "Easier than trying to balance plates on our knees in the parlor, don't you agree?" She rearranged the settings while she directed John to place an extra chair next to me.

"I understand you've been birding." Graham bent close to me as he sat, brushing my shoulder with his, but his smile went around the table and managed to include Andrew and John in his remark. "I suppose you've already told the whole story, but would it bore you too much to tell me as well?"

Andrew was only too willing, and Graham was soon laughing at our version of John's birdsongs. "I've seen and heard the petrels, and I've also seen John's act. A remarkable resemblance between the two, I'd say."

John bowed his head, the deepening color of his wind-scoured cheeks acknowledging the compliment.

"It was a marvelous day for me," I said. "What I don't understand, though, is how we got there. We followed the path, that was easy enough. Then we left it, turning toward the sea at just the right place. But I could see no sign that this was right, or see what John saw that told him this way was safe."

"Ach," said John, cryptic as always, "you canna always see, so you must learn to listen."

I thought of the noise on the cliff, the birds crying, the wind blowing, the swell breaking and splashing against the rocks. There must be times when the noise would be even greater. Listen? Listen to what?

Graham said, "If you went to the hermitage you must have seen John's tomb as well. Have they shown you their treasure from it?"

John said, "I'm no certain the lass would like to see it."

A general cry of disbelief rang around the table. "Of course she would," said an incredulous Andrew. "Our something special. Wouldn't you?" He turned to me for confirmation.

John spoke again, softly. "Isabel didn't approve that we'd emptied the tomb."

"Not you. You didn't empty it," said Johanna.

"All the same. The lass thinks it wrong, and happen she could be right."

"It isn't so much that I don't approve." I felt relieved we were talking about it. John had forgiven me, but without letting me explain. "It's just that—I suppose I thought of my father and his grave, and how I'd feel if it were opened and his...he..." I stopped, my throat tightening with grief. I couldn't refer to my father as merely bones.

"But those people aren't here anymore," Johanna said, "not the people who made the graves, nor those whose forebears are buried there, not that anyone knows. There's no one left to remember them, to care."

Like Thora, I thought, as I had at Hamehollow. Not so many years from now most of us around this table would be gone, us, and Bea and Ivor as well, and who then would remember her? Would anyone know that this young girl once lived here, this self-invented witch, who tried, in her own remarkable way, to save the earth? Would even Andrew remember more than a fascination tinged with fright, and a dim sorrow? But I only said, "Yes. John explained all that. All the same, I thought they should stay where they'd been placed."

"They'd all soon be in the sea, then," Andrew declared. His stern, pompous demeanor matched his words, if not his youthful face. "You must have seen that. Uncle John didn't look for the grave, to rob it or to harm it. He just found it, by accident, and then he rescued it."

"Yes, you're right. I know that now. And I'd like to see what you have from it, I think."

But they were enjoying their discussion now, and were not easily turned from it. Oddly, this talk of graves seemed to remind no one but me of Thora.

"Many things we've found in these islands in that way," said Nan, "by accident. We've found them while gathering stones, or digging for something else."

"Aye," John said. "Or by accident pure and simple, in its rightful sense. A farmer not so far from here found an ancient grave once while plowing his field. A hole appeared of a sudden, right beneath his tractor. Half fell in himself, he did—into an early grave you might say." John laughed, clearly enjoying his own joke.

"The sea, too, exposes many sites," Graham said when the laughter ended, his pedantic manner restoring seriousness, "as it would have John's tomb before long, had John not found it first. And sometimes the wind exposes what it once buried long ago. We certainly don't have to search for antiquities here, not as they do in other places. We've many more. Since we have so few trees, our past is all in stone, though even stone is not eternal, and may wash or crumble away. And so much of our past is out in the open, a part of the land."

"The standing stones, you mean."

"Or Maes Howe. Even covered, as it is, with sod, no one could mistake it for a natural feature of the landscape."

"So it was plundered."

"Aye, by the Vikings. And as they were among our ancestors, I suppose we must share some of the blame. But wouldn't you, if you'd found something long buried, long forgotten? Wouldn't you be curious? Wouldn't you look?"

"Look, yes. But didn't they take—"

"Who knows what they took, or why?" Nan said quietly.

Andrew shook his head, a look of wistful regret on his face. "They say there was no treasure."

"Not for them, probably," said Graham. "The Vikings had their own ideas of what constituted treasure, and certainly human remains would not have qualified. Today, I'm not so sure. We've laws to protect our antiquities, but some will always get around them. Collectors now will pay huge sums for things we might imagine could only find homes in museums: gravestones, runic carvings, tiny beads, pot shards."

And Viking treasure. As Ross had known.

"But a boy found a treasure." Andrew brightened. "A real treasure. A Viking hoard."

"A boy?" I said, still thinking of Ross, and Ben Gowan. "You must mean—"

"At Skail Bay," Graham put in quickly. "Many years ago. Near Skara Brae. You've visited Skara Brae, surely."

I shook my head. "Not yet. I haven't had the chance."

"You must. I'll take you there myself. Not a grave site, so there's no question of interfering with sacred remains. But an entire Stone Age village, the houses preserved just as the inhabitants left them in the middle of their daily lives. It was the wind that uncovered it for us, as perhaps it was the wind that buried it in the first place. But not before adequate warning, as no evidence was found of mortality. Or of battles. One would expect the people should have returned, but they did not, or at any event, not after that final time. A local climate change occurred perhaps, violent storms in a previously calm bay. There is evidence of occupation over long periods, however, as beneath those houses we've uncovered stand even earlier ones."

"There, you see!" Johanna said triumphantly. "Even the ancients didn't preserve things as they were, just because they'd always been that way. They built new houses on top of old, whole villages—"

"Aye, and shifted burial remains as well," finished Graham. "The tomb was sacred, but not static. In many, whole skeletons are found in one chamber, while disarticulated bones are in another. Often incomplete remains of several individuals, these bones had been moved long after interment, to make room, it seems, for newer burials. Sometimes, probably as a result of particular funerary practices and certain religious beliefs, one chamber will contain only skulls, while another only long bones, and so on."

We had come back, full circle, to graves.

"Burial customs are mostly for the living, I think," Nan said. "And the parts that are for the dead are meant to ensure a happy afterlife. Perhaps it isn't right, and after all, who can say? But it seems to me 'twould be a grand afterlife to end up in a museum five thousand years from now. I'd love to think I'll be telling folk all about my world long after I'm gone from it."

"Aye," said John, "we need to know who came before us. And those who come after will need to know about us. Now we have books to tell our stories, but there's more to history than just words. Those before us had only stone, and pots, and beads, and bones. But happen the lass could be right, after all. Happen we shouldn't be the ones to decide what to dig, what to take. But it's been done, hasn't it, and years ago now."

"But what is it that you have from your tomb that you won't show me?" The discussion had wound to a natural end. This seemed the right time to ask.

"May we show it to her, please?" begged Andrew.

He didn't wait for agreement, but took me by the hand and led me, followed by the others, into the front room. Surrounded by the soft cushions and books and sheet music, Thora's blue and cream weaving still cascaded from the piano top. I carefully kept my eyes from it. I was enjoying the past now. The present would intrude itself again soon enough.

Andrew still held my hand. He led me to a straight-backed chair. "Now sit ye down," he said, sounding exactly like Uncle John.

John had opened a glass-fronted cabinet, and came back cradling something in his hands. He placed it gently in my lap.

It was a human skull.

I took it in my own hands. It was cool and smooth, smaller than I would have imagined, and a soft, mottled ocher color, like the eggs I sometimes bought from a farm where the hens ranged free and scratched and chuckled underfoot in the farmyard. There was nothing repellent about it. The empty eye sockets stared up at me without emotion. There was nothing there to elicit horror.

It was simply and straightforwardly human. If anything, I felt a serenity from it, the easiness of close family contact.

The skull belonged to a young woman, they told me. Who was she? How had she died? Had she lived long enough to bear children? Was it possible that we here could be descended from her, one of us, or all? Across five thousand years I felt a kinship with this small sphere of bones.

I put a hand on my stomach and imagined, impossibly, that I felt movement there. But though it was much too soon for that, this life inside me was real. How could I think of ending it? For that moment, at least, I could not. I envisioned myself as a guardian of a chain connecting the skull to the present and then beyond, a circle—no, a spiral of life.

I looked at the faces waiting expectantly for my reaction. I'd been wrong about the tomb. As John said, we needed to know who came before us. We needed to have archaeologists study what we could find of the past, and tell us how it was. I thought again of Thora, and her ritualistic links with the past. We all needed those connections, through myth, through family histories, through community identities, and, if we were truly fortunate, through personal participation like this.

"They let us keep it, that one thing," said John. "All else they took to Edinburgh. But this, 'twas one of a jumble of bones, a part they couldn't match with any other, don't you see. So 'tis ours, to help us remember what we had."

"It would fit perfectly into my museum, but they refuse to give it to me," Graham complained good-naturedly.

Despite John's defense of the emptied tomb from which the skull had come, his reply didn't really surprise me. "Better for it to be here, to be close," he said, "for that skull and for all the others. The dead. So they can remember where they'd been."

*　*　*

It was not yet seven o'clock, and the sun, finally emerging from its cover of cloud, raked long streaks of watery light across the floor of the room, but Nan was yawning and Andrew had fallen asleep in his chair. Graham drove me home.

"If you're not too tired—" Graham began as we drove past the dark, still form of my father's cottage, then interrupted himself. "That's quite a walk, John's grand tour. It wearied Andrew, and he's accustomed to it."

"Yes. I'm tired, too. But I feel better after today. About Thora, I mean. And my father. We've talked for hours about graves and I've held a skull in my hands, yet I feel consoled somehow."

Graham nodded. "Aye. The past helps us to accept sometimes. And in distress, it doesn't matter what you do, or what you talk about. Being with friends in itself brings solace."

He let the silence lie between us for a while, then said again, "If you're not too tired . . . it's early still. Why not come home with me? To Sinclair House, that is," he added hastily.

To his museum, not to his home. I heard the discomfiture in his voice as he too swiftly clarified his meaning.

"We've a few things there I know you'll like to see. No skulls, nor other bones, but Viking artifacts. We normally keep them under lock and key, in glass cases for general viewing. But I could take them out for you. You could hold them, see them closely now."

Instead of going back too soon to my lonely room, where yesterday's horrors might return. "Yes," I said, "I'd like that."

Sinclair House sat in a hollow, with small hills rising and falling away from it in all directions. Short, gnarled trees grew against the walls surrounding the house, their rustling leaves making noises that already sounded alien to my ears.

"Our grove." Graham laughed at my surprise. "We're protected from the stronger winds here. My grandfather planted these trees, and as they've survived this long, no doubt they'll survive forever— or at least for my lifetime. Come in."

He had unlocked the door with several keys, and we entered a wide hall dominated by a large antique desk topped with a modern telephone, surrounded by commercial racks holding maps, guidebooks, and local histories for sale.

"I live upstairs. But in here..." Graham led me through a Victorian room of stuffed birds in chests and on tables, and small stuffed animals on shelves, to another room furnished only with glass cases.

"This is our Viking room. Some exhibits are copies, though most are genuine." He unlocked one of the cases and withdrew a small silver box with a ridged, peaked lid. "Like this casket, for example."

"Casket?"

"Chest, then. The term is often misunderstood. It is not necessarily funerary, although the one that Ben Gowan found might well have been, since frequently the Vikings made cenotaphs, or memorial burials. There was concern, when someone was lost at sea, for example, that the person's spirit might not find his heaven, or that the gods might not find him. Or that they might forget his name. Someone, a father or a son, or a friend, perhaps, would inscribe a stone with the dead man's name, and place it at a crossroads where everyone would see, and remember. Sometimes under the stone they buried a few of his precious belongings, things that might otherwise have gone to the grave with him or been burned on a pyre."

The practice was not so odd, nor so archaic as it seemed at first. I thought of the Vietnam Veterans' Memorial. The granite wall proclaimed name after name of the dead, and people searched for them, and found them, and ran their fingers over those incised names. They left flowers against the wall below them, or photographs, a baseball glove, a pair of boots. Wasn't it the same?

Graham continued. "But this casket we have here was empty,

and I believe was not one of those. It was found with a helmet and a cart."

He set aside the casket, along with a small modern glass box that held an age-darkened leather cloche, then brought out a long, curved, sculpted wooden form.

"Unfortunately, this portion is all that remains of the cart."

The broken end that had once been attached to the cart was worn black and smooth with time. The other end narrowed and swelled and curved into the shape of a fantastic animal head, with huge eyes and a snarling, toothed mouth. From end to end the wood was elaborately carved in a tiny, intricate pattern that repeated variations of itself over and over again to cover the whole surface—small men or animals with sinuous, intertwining limbs, hands and feet grasping at everything near. Their many faces stared out at me with large familiar eyes.

The room began to spin, and I drew in my breath with a gasp Graham must have heard.

"I see you recognize the carving on the dragon," I heard Graham's lecturer's voice carry on, humming in my head, in a room that was suddenly empty of air, "or at least its fine artistry. This was the most popular of the Viking motifs. It's from the Borre period, and it represents the best of Viking art. It's called *the gripping beast.*"

Seventeen

Is't known who did this more than bloody deed?
—MACBETH, ACT II, SCENE iv

Thora was murdered," I blurted out to Constable MacFee. I'd planned my words differently as I drove to the police house late the next morning. I was going to begin at the beginning and tell him everything that had happened, everything I'd noticed. I'd planned not to say those words at all at first, but to lead MacFee himself to that conclusion.

Probably he'd come to it already on his own. Probably he'd known it all along. He responded by raising his eyebrows and drawing up a chair for me as he had a few days ago.

The room looked the same as it had then: the desk with its papers and telephone, the lists and notices on the bulletin board, the large-scale map of Digerness on the wall. MacFee looked the same, too, with his neat white shirt and dark tie under his uniform pullover, his concerned, unrevealing face. Only I was different. Today I was confident. Today I had no doubts.

I had stared at the Viking dragon's head in Graham's museum

the night before and, instead of a dragon, saw in its carved design the brooch pinning the riotous tartan kilt sash to Thora's breast, the brooch whose many eyes had dazzled me while her hurtling words had overwhelmed me. And I saw that sash fluttering unpinned over Thora's body. I'd heard, without really listening to, the hum of Graham's voice while he talked on about Viking art, about its rise to and decline from the spirited gripping beast motif. He had taken my silence for interest, or for awe, perhaps of the artifacts, perhaps of his knowledge. I became dimly aware that he'd laid aside the length of the wooden cart and moved closer to me. I heard his softly whispered, "Isabel."

Still consumed with the image of the gripping beast, convinced that Thora's brooch had been just that, pondering what Thora's possession of it might mean, I stepped thoughtlessly away from him. I hardly noticed his kiss landing somewhere behind my ear. When, my head still whirling with the sense of what I'd seen, I said, "Please, Graham, take me home," his stiffened, arched response only deepened my abstraction. For in that moment he was like nothing more than the frustrated, indignant Ross MacDonald on Hamehollow. Ross, who had "wooed" me only to conceal his pursuit of a Viking treasure.

Graham's strained, courteous conversation accompanied us all the way back to the inn.

In the morning, to my surprise, Ivor Denison had joined me at my breakfast table. He sat without saying a word. His stern demeanor hadn't changed. Even his face looked much the same, the haggard lines around his eyes, the only indications of anguish, hardly visible behind his glasses.

"You found her," he said after a time.

"Yes."

"I come to you as a representative of Furrowend. We wish to express our regrets for your distressing experience, and offer our aid should there be any we can give you."

"Thank you." What more could I say in response to such a formal, dispassionate speech? I wasn't sure he'd welcome my offer of sympathy, but under the circumstances I was more than likely the only one who would give it. "This must be even more distressing for you," I said.

He stared at me blankly for a second, then dropped his eyes. When he spoke his voice quavered. "She stayed away deliberately. She wanted me to mention her at the ceremony, to publicly acknowledge her contribution to our victory over nuclear waste. How could I do such a thing? My position, my—" He let it drop. "I refused, of course." He raised his head. "So our last words were in anger."

He stood. "It will help no one to tell any of this to anyone. So you will say nothing. Understand?" And he turned and walked away.

Meggie had been watching us, her face rumpled with concern. Was her concern for me or her father? Meggie could already be aware of more than Ivor thought.

By ten I was in Kirkwall, in the library. I searched through books of Vikings and books of Viking art, looking for a photograph of a round gold brooch depicting gripping beasts. I found four of them, none exactly like Thora's, but all of them with the same symmetry of faces, the same intricately contorted bodies, the same artful conception. More convinced than ever that a master craftsman, ancient or contemporary, had executed her brooch, I knew then I had to speak to Constable MacFee once more.

Now MacFee's eyebrows were still raised, his eyes on mine, waiting for me to go on.

"When I found her I didn't question her death, didn't think about anything except that it was the wall that killed her. I thought she'd climbed onto it to perform one of her rituals and fell. Precarious places attracted her." Like the solitary monk of the hermitage. "Religious places, too, for her performances. She saw her rites as kinds of sacraments, I think, in her secret, sacred places."

MacFee cocked his head inquisitively. "You seem to know much about Thora."

"She told me some. I thought of her as being theatrical. She thought of herself as a sort of intermediary with nature. She believed, through her magic, she could use nature and control it. She seemed to ignore the danger of her places. It may even have been a vital element to her sorcery. Andrew told me—"

"Andrew?"

"Sorry. Andrew MacLeod, a young boy from Inverness. He and his mother visit at Otterness Farm each summer. He knew Thora, was intrigued by her. He saw her last year out on the hermitage near the farm."

I paused. MacFee indicated with a slight movement of his head that he knew the place. Still, I hesitated. I was about to break Andrew's confidence. I closed my eyes and silently asked his forgiveness.

Then I spoke. "He saw her dancing a ritual on the hermitage. He was frightened by it, especially since she ran back across the bridge completely unconcerned about slipping and falling. When Andrew told me about that, I was certain that she'd finally fallen. If she'd been dancing on the hermitage, why not at Hamehollow? And the wall was crumbling and unsafe, Ross said."

Ross. A few days ago I'd accused him of trying to kill me. Was I now going to accuse him of killing Thora? I was sure Thora had died because of the treasure. But I couldn't believe that Ross could have stood beside her, could have looked into her face, and struck her dead.

She didn't fall. I had imagined her swaying on the wall's thin, uneven course, reeling in a bewitched ecstasy, teetering, her long kilt wrapping her and capturing her legs, losing her balance, being pitched to the sharp ground. But she had removed her clothes for her ritual at the hermitage. Had she been dancing here she would have done the same. I asked MacFee, "Was she pushed from the wall? Or was she hit?"

I didn't expect an answer, but his shoulders lifted and fell instead of his eyebrows. "We don't know yet. But rest assured, we've combed the site carefully, with the help of Kirkwall and Inverness. We'll set up a fully equipped murder enquiry office if we hear from Aberdeen that we must. Everything we've found has gone to Aberdeen, you see. Photos, possible weapons, all the evidence."

"And Thora?"

"Aye."

The memory washed over me. I smelled again the bitter, pungent smell of the blood mixed with the sweet smell of the heather. I felt again my disbelieving horror when I touched the unyielding flesh of Thora's cheek.

I put my head down on my knees.

MacFee sprang up from his chair, and soon knelt by my side.

"I'm all right." As I sat up, my eyes were caught by his police badge, and for a horrifying moment I imagined that it, too, encircled the images of the gripping beast. Then I saw that its intertwining design was controlled and geometric, that its lines were not limbs, that it contained no leering faces.

"Are you certain?" MacFee studied my face, then took his time going around his desk and resettling in his chair. "Then I must ask. You say you thought she'd fallen. Yet you tell me now you're sure she's been murdered, pushed or struck. What made you change your mind?"

I took a deep breath, let it out, and started at the beginning.

"Early on the day she died I went to her studio." I pulled the *Orkneyinga Saga* from my jacket pocket and slid it across the desk to MacFee. "While I was here Monday night, Thora, or someone, left this for me at the inn."

He bent his head to the book, but didn't pick it up.

"I told you that she'd warned me of danger the day we met. The book was meant to be another omen, I thought. Possibly even a threat. A bookmark came with it, one Thora had made."

"They do sell them at the craft shop," MacFee said reasonably. Thora had said the same thing herself.

"But it was in the book, marking the story about the death of Earl Harald. About Helga and Frakkok. Do you know it?"

"Aye."

"They were witches. They worked in fabric."

"Like Thora," MacFee agreed. "And the bookmark, you say, was at that page?"

"Yes." I nodded, but I could feel the lie visible in my eyes. "I'm certain it was. I pulled it out before I noted exactly where, but when I reached that page, I knew for certain. The passages are underlined, and what's most convincing, I think, a warning of danger is written there. So I went to see her."

"You knew? What did you know?"

"That the book had come from Thora. That she was using it to tell me something. Or to frighten me away."

"And she admitted that?"

"No. But she'd done it before. And she'd rammed into me. I told you about that."

"Aye. We found your witnesses. And it appears you're probably correct, she did attack you." He turned his head away momentarily and sighed, the only emotion he'd shown. "But we'd had no chance to speak with Thora herself."

I nodded, silent myself for a moment, and went on. "Thora was doing something, though she admitted to nothing. I'm certain now it was to do with Ross's treasure hunt. Surely it's too much to believe that missing Viking gold and a dead woman are unconnected. Unless you believe in her powers, that she really had felt danger for me." The uneasy thought that had lingered at the edges of my grief came back. Danger for me, or danger from me?

"We know why Ross thought you involved, but why should Thora?" MacFee asked. "Why should she try to rid us of you? She told you nothing more?"

"Nothing. She raved about her magic. She intimidated me. That's when I saw she was wearing a brooch. The day she died she was wearing a brooch that I'm certain was a part of the Viking hoard."

MacFee no longer looked imperturbable. When he repeated back my words it was with a question, though I knew he knew the answer. "The Viking hoard?"

"Ross's. Ben Gowan's. The design was Viking, I just learned last night. And this morning, at the library. A design called the gripping beast." As I described the brooch to him I saw it yet again, the staring, strangled faces in the liquid gleam of gold. "And it was gold. Where would Thora get real gold?"

MacFee looked skeptical. "If it was, as you say, part of the hoard, what was she doing with it? More likely for her to have ordinary real gold than something such as that."

"I don't know. But it may be the reason she died. Because you didn't find it on her body at Hamehollow, did you?"

He didn't reply. But from the closed look on his face, I knew he hadn't.

I said, "She wore it that morning. If she'd simply taken it off, she'd have replaced it with another, wouldn't she? That morning it pinned her kilt sash. Nothing pinned it, no brooch of any kind, when I found her at Hamehollow. No gold, no gripping beast."

"So you believe she had the treasure, and Ross MacDonald killed her to acquire it?"

I spread my hands, waiting for MacFee to offer his own answer. He offered only silence.

To make an accusation, even to offer an opinion, was a terrible responsibility. Yet the whole mystery came back to Ross.

Or possibly to one other person. I'd put off saying anything as long as I could, not because Ivor Denison had ordered me to keep his secret—I'd intended all along to tell—but because until this morning I had almost agreed with him.

Almost. Unless a whim had become an embarrassment. Unless Thora had begun demanding more from the relationship than he was prepared to give.

"There's one more thing," I told MacFee. "Thora was seeing someone secretly. Ivor Denison, of Furrowend. Meggie's father."

Again expressionless, he said, "How do you know?"

"I saw them meet, and kiss. He told me not to tell anyone."

Once more Constable MacFee said nothing. I'd said all I'd come to say. I'd told him all I knew. I got up to leave.

Then I stopped. The night I found Thora's body, Constable MacFee had questioned me. I remembered his words. "No other cars there? Coming or going?" There hadn't been, and there had been no car parked with mine, or at the bottom of the hill. There had been no green Beetle anywhere in sight.

"If it was an accident, how did she get there?" I asked MacFee now.

"Aye," he said. "We've taken that into consideration. We've taken in her car as well. I think we've thought of everything." His face softened. "You're concerned, I understand that, and only trying to help. But don't worry." He came from around his desk. I thought he would shake my hand, but instead he put an arm around my shoulder and gave me a comforting pat. "You're a stranger here. You've done all you can. Your involvement in this problem has been incidental, no matter how it seems. You've nothing to fear. You were right to come to me today. Thank you for your information. We appreciate your help. We'll take care of everything from now on. We'll do our best. And our best will be to find out what happened, I promise."

* * *

White clouds were mounding on the horizon before a stiffening wind. Just a few days ago Graham had waited for me here, leaning idly against his car in warm bars of sun. I missed his steadfast presence. I wished he were waiting for me now, ready to walk with me and comfort me, but last night I'd managed to drive him away.

As I got into my car it occurred to me that while Graham had been waiting here, Ross was telling MacFee and me about the treasure.

I sat there recalling yesterday at Otterness. I'd almost said something about Ben Gowan's treasure. Graham had jumped in, as though he'd known what I was about to say, and prevented me from saying it. Then, last night, he'd referred to the casket Ben Gowan had found, had revealed he knew it had not been empty. How did he know?

I glanced back at the solid stone building. Could Graham have been listening to Ross? Could he have overheard? I wanted to walk back to the police house, to stand with my ear to the door or the window. But I wouldn't hear anyone talking now. And MacFee, already doubtful of me, might find me there.

Why hadn't Graham just told me he knew about the treasure, instead of inviting me to Sinclair House and showing me the gripping beast design? He may have wanted to learn if I could identify it, to find out if I'd seen Thora's brooch and recognized it for what it was.

But Graham wasn't Ross. Graham was trying to please me, not follow me. It was coincidence that he'd shown me the gripping beast. Even if he'd known about Ben Gowan's casket, he hadn't necessarily seen its contents. He couldn't have known about the brooch.

The only way to be sure was to ask.

I had no problem finding the road to Sinclair House, or the house itself, nestled in its own small forest. But I didn't find Graham there. A stern woman at the ornate desk offered to sell me admittance to the museum, but could only tell me that Graham had left hours before for Kirkwall.

It doesn't matter, I told myself. MacFee was right. I'm a stranger here, a tourist. I've done all I could. What did Graham know? What did Ross know? MacFee would learn the truth.

I had my own work, and I'd been neglecting it. I went to Kirkwall myself, for the second time that day.

I sat across the street from St. Magnus Cathedral to draw the twelfth-century church, an ancient monument to be sure, but a vital church, still in daily use.

Its steeple pierced a rapidly darkening sky. Despite the growing dark and the rising wind, people crisscrossed the deep lawns in front of it, sprawled on the grass or the benches. Children played. Tubs of red petunias, garish in the gray light, were all that separated the happy crowds from the graveyards flanking the Cathedral.

I crossed Broad Street and went inside. I had heard that the bones of St. Magnus the Martyr were immured in one of the red Gothic pillars, or alternatively, in a section of the altar. I didn't seek them out. Instead, I studied the weathered, ancient gravestones that now stood against the walls beneath the Gothic arches of the nave.

These were monuments of a more accepting, less romantic time. *Momento Mori*, their once-chiseled faces declared pragmatically, instead of words of hope to offer to the living. Death's heads surmounted them, instead of winged cherubs to watch over the dead. Had they been brought inside so as not to affront modern mourners in the churchyard, or simply because they had broken and fallen, and had so eroded as to require rescue to the interior?

Of course they'd once stood outside. I knew they'd suffered wind and rain in the churchyard, but I wanted to believe they'd been in this sanctuary forever. I wanted to believe that the storms that had nearly erased the names of those forgotten dead had raged not from the heavens, but from the tormented hearts of living mortals, praying in the pews.

Last night, holding the skull, I'd felt the continuity of life, of my own place in the long history of man. I'd longed to be a part of it. But with the morning had come the reality of death and life, and I thought again about giving a lifetime of care to another person, requiring skills I knew I did not have, and I considered once more going home to end my pregnancy.

I sat for a time in a pew and joined my own heart into the maelstrom.

Outside, the air was heavy with moisture. I tried to add a few more completed pages to my sketchbook before the rain began. Around the corner, on Watergate, I worked at sketches of the ruins of the Bishop's Palace. I tried to suggest the former glory once housed by its scoured walls and its round tower. Across the street, I drew the Earl's Palace, its magnificence still evident in its wood carvings, in the rounded bays of its oriel windows and the decorative stonework on their corbeled undersides.

Beyond a crumpled wall I saw the Cathedral spire, and the rose window below it. I tried to draw that, too, but the Kirkwall Police Station intruded its ominous, neighboring presence into my subconscious. When I looked down at my sketchbook and saw that I'd drawn what I'd imagined in Constable MacFee's office—a Northern Constabulary police badge with tortuous gripping beasts forming its center—I collected my car to go home.

Even on the town streets the wind grabbed and shook my car. I drove slowly back down Broad Street. The sky loomed black behind the red stones of St. Magnus Cathedral.

The lawns were deserted. One lonely figure huddled on a sidewalk bench in front of the Cathedral wall. I recognized the face peering from the clutched, hooded coat. Bea MacDonald sat waiting for a bus.

Eighteen

Ring the alarum bell! Blow, wind! come, wrack!
—MACBETH, ACT V, SCENE V

I turned the car as soon as I could and pulled to the curb, leaning over to roll down the passenger-side window. "Mrs. MacDonald. Can I give you a ride home?"

Bea MacDonald raised her head and peered suspiciously toward me. The unfamiliar car, its interior dark against the eerie glow of the storm light, must have obscured my identity. But even as recognition smoothed her puzzled forehead, Bea began to shake her head no.

Abruptly, the rain began. Huge drops, as visible as snowflakes, pelted down. The few people still on the streets dashed for cover, and Bea MacDonald changed her mind.

She scurried to the car. I should have helped her, but the situation had changed too suddenly for my befuddled mind. I should have rushed out, opened the door, and helped her in. Her movements looked stiff and painful as she stooped slowly into the car. Her gnarled fingers could barely curl around the door handle to pull it closed. As we pulled away I saw that they now twisted together in a restive clasp in her lap. Where was Ross? What was Bea doing so far from home without him, depending on the bus on a day like this?

"I've been praying," she said, as though I'd asked aloud.

I tore my eyes from the windshield, now awash with rain, to look at Bea's face, expecting to see some smug expression, some challenging smile after this startling display of mind-reading. Was this what Nan had meant when she'd called Bea a bit fey?

But Bea's face showed nothing, except possibly a glimmer of piety. She stared down into her hands, and after a brief time opened them, as if to release a prayer still lingering there.

"I've been to St. Magnus. I've been praying."

"At the Cathedral? Instead of St. Anne's?" Wouldn't St. Anne's be where she'd go to pray, especially on a day like today? But the bus might not run to the little church at the end of the narrow lane in Digerness, where I'd guided my fingertips over my father's initials, carved like runic inscriptions into the aged, smooth wood of the pew. And where I'd watched a family, indeed a whole community, eagerly welcome a child into its lifelong care.

"Aye, St. Anne's is my parish church," Bea was saying, "and hers as well. But I've been to St. Magnus himself, you see. To pray for her soul."

"For Thora." I nodded, understanding. Nan had also said that Bea had spun wool for Thora. She'd suggested that Thora and Bea were friends despite the difference in their ages. They had worked together in the co-op. Bea herself had shown concern for Thora at the Festival, had talked about taking her soup for her supper.

"He's there, you know," Bea continued, interrupting my thoughts. "In the Cathedral. The bones of St. Magnus are right there, sealed up inside the altar, and they make miracles even to this day."

The rain came heavier now. The windshield wipers slashed

back and forth ineffectually, the clear swaths they made lasting scarcely long enough for me to see my way directly ahead. Although the rain beat at us from straight on, the wind blew from all directions. It tossed the car from side to side, and sometimes seemed to lift us completely off the road for minutes at a time. I slowed to a crawl.

I clung to the steering wheel and hunched myself over it, as though being closer to the windshield would allow me to see better through it. I tried to concentrate wholly on my driving, but Bea MacDonald's bent figure kept demanding my attention, crowding itself into my sight. My eyes staring straight ahead, I still saw her, supplicant and sad, beside me.

"I'm sorry," I managed to say when we finally turned off the main road. The smaller road was nearer to Digerness, and not as traveled. We were less likely to meet other vehicles blindly head-on. I was able to relax at last, enough to offer this small condolence. At the edge of my vision I saw Bea straighten and nod, then sink back into her prayerful attitude.

I envied Bea her easy faith in St. Magnus, if she was truly receiving comfort from it. Perhaps I should go back to St. Anne's. Would I find such comfort there? But Bea's faith was more accepting than mine. And Bea had not found Thora's body, did not see it still each time she closed her eyes. Nor had Bea quarreled with Thora on the morning of her death. She wouldn't be berating herself for bringing on Thora's headache, for making Thora miss the Festival.

But grief comes to each of us in its own way, unique, incomparable. Bea was grieving for her friend.

"I'm sure you'll be lonely without her," I said.

"Aye," said Bea. She closed her eyes for a moment, then sat up straighter in her seat. When she spoke again her voice was more cheerful. "But I'll soon have Meggie, who'll be Ross's bride, and she'll have wee bairns to fill the house."

Suddenly she leaned forward and cried, "There!"

I slammed on the brakes. I fought the car to a straight, smooth stop, only to see that the road before us held no hazard, no stalled vehicle to crash into, no wayward sheep or cattle. Then I spied my father's cottage.

"That's where I'll be living," Bea said calmly. "Ross and Meggie will occupy my farmhouse, and I'll have this cottage. 'Tis just the right size for me alone. You've seen it. My brother began the repairs, you see, and now that he's gone, Ross will carry on."

But he wouldn't, I was afraid. Poor Bea. She would not live in a neat stone cottage with swallows in its chimney, with her grandchildren nearby. No matter what happened, she would lose her son. Even if Ross had not killed Thora, he would probably soon find the treasure. He might already have done so. After all, if Thora had a part of it, it was not difficult to believe he could have the rest. Bea would see him jailed, or would watch him sail off on the *St. Ola* to a new life in Edinburgh or London.

"He's gone, just now, to Edinburgh."

Poor Bea, poor fey Bea. It was all an illusion. She might seem to read my mind, but she hadn't done it properly, not this time. Not these thoughts. And I didn't think she would ever read the thoughts of her son.

At Bea MacDonald's farmhouse I got out first, went around, and offered my arm to Bea. During the slow negotiation of the short distance between the car and the rear entrance to the house, the driving rain soaked us both. Inside, Bea peeled off her jacket, draped it, still dripping, on a hook beside the door, and sank wearily into a kitchen chair. She gave a short, violent shiver. Would it be all right to leave her alone?

I stood just inside the doorway, waiting, my jacket hanging heavy and cold across my shoulders, the denim of my jeans plastered against my legs, wondering when Ross had gone to Edinburgh. And when—or if—he would return.

I noticed the tea things precisely laid out on a lace-edged cloth on an old-fashioned kitchen dresser: the electric kettle, the round, brown teapot, a bowl of teabags in their small green envelopes. At the sight of them I became aware of the quivering chill inside me, of the gooseflesh under my wet clothes. Tea promised warmth for both of us. Moreover, it promised conversation. And information about Ross and what he might be up to.

"Let me make you a cup of tea," I offered.

But perhaps Bea still read my mind after all. She looked appraisingly around at her own neat kitchen. "Ach, I can manage well enough alone," she said. She pushed herself up, walked over to me, and reached around me to open the door we'd just found haven through. "I've tablets to take for my joints, you see. Like magic, they work. You take yourself off now. I'm grateful for the lift, but I need no more assistance."

Manipulating the car back to the inn, I bombarded myself with the questions Bea hadn't allowed me to ask. What reason had Ross given for going to Edinburgh? A day's trip by sea and road to Inverness, then the next day's train to Edinburgh—or an impossibly expensive flight—was not a trip taken lightly from Orkney. Had MacFee allowed him to leave? Did MacFee even know that he'd gone? Did Ross intend to return, or had he fled forever?

Did Bea know the answers? She was not there to read my mind. No one answered me.

I worried myself through dinner. I pushed the food around on my plate, unaware of what it was, leaving most of it. I sat alone in the television lounge afterward, between a rain-washed window and the sweltering fireplace. Wind howled down the chimney, slapped the shutters against the walls, and rattled the windowpanes. Rain battered against the windows, sometimes mixed with a sharp barrage of hail. Thunder rumbled. Yet, however fierce, these were the sounds of shelter, of a storm kept at a distance, and they drowned out the workaday sounds of the inn. I drifted into an uneasy sleep.

I dreamed about Ben Gowan. He kept changing in appearance. Sometimes he looked exactly like Ross, but I knew he was Ben Gowan. Sometimes he looked exactly like Bea MacDonald. He seemed angry with me, telling me over and over that I couldn't have the treasure, that it belonged to the dead. But he showed me Graham's Viking dragon's head, and a silver and carved ivory casket. He opened the casket to draw out Thora's gripping beast brooch, to hold it out to me. And all the while he kept saying to me, "It isn't yours. You'll never find it. It belongs to the dead."

I tried to tell him I didn't want it, I wasn't looking for it. Why did everyone keep insisting I was searching for the treasure?

All the others were there, everyone I'd met in Orkney.

I pleaded with each of them in turn, "Tell him I'm not looking for the treasure. She has it." I pointed to Thora, sitting at her loom weaving. Her brilliant hair tumbled over her face, hiding her terrible wound, but drops of blood dripped from it onto her work.

They all stared blankly at me, as though they didn't hear. Only Ross spoke. He turned to Graham, pointed at him, and said, "Sinclair isn't allowed here. This is none of his affair. He must leave."

Graham left, but I couldn't see him go, or determine just how far away he went. I only heard the door open, saw Ross's satisfied smile, and heard it close again.

I studied each of their faces. Ben Gowan had hidden the treasure, then died. Thora had learned its hiding place, and had taken it for herself. Now Thora was dead. But Ben Gowan and Thora were both here now. Was Thora's killer here, too?

Someone was shaking me.

"Isabel. Miss Garth. I'm sorry to bother you."

I opened my eyes, expecting to see a room full of dream people, a room full of ghosts, but only Meggie was there, stooping over me.

"I'm sorry to wake you, but you're wanted downstairs on the telephone. 'Tis Johanna MacLeod. 'Tis urgent, she says."

Still partly engulfed in the dream, I followed Meggie slowly down the stairs to the phone on her desk.

Johanna's voice, shrill and breathless, cried through heavy static on the line. "Isabel, please, is he with you? Have you seen him? We can't find him anywhere. Isabel, I don't know what we're going to do."

Her voice rose higher and broke into a wail. "Oh, God, Andrew is missing!"

Nineteen

O horror, horror, horror! Tongue nor heart
Cannot conceive nor name thee.
—MACBETH, ACT II, SCENE iii

Thunder shook the air, and the phone went dead.

I sat staring at the lifeless handpiece as though willing it to tell me all the things Johanna had not. Andrew missing? When? How? I was afraid to ask, even of myself, why? My hand trembled, so that when I finally replaced the receiver it made a loud clatter into the brittle silence of the room.

I noticed for the first time that the restaurant doors were closed, that the only light in the lobby came from the night-lights. I looked at my watch. It was past eleven, but for a summer night, uncommonly dark.

The wind still raged, howling and rattling against the windows and doors, but the rain and hail had stopped temporarily. At least Andrew was not lost somewhere in that torrential rain.

And he was only lost. I refused to admit Thora into my mind, to make the smallest connection between her death and Andrew's disappearance.

I would be of no help at the farm. How could I search for Andrew when I didn't know my own way, when I wasn't even sure I could find the farm in the dark? But I couldn't stay here doing nothing. At least I could offer comfort. I had to go to Otterness.

My headlights pierced the darkness and shimmered back off the wet road. The wind flung an occasional brief, hard spate of leftover rain against the windshield and battered the car from side to side. I inched forward through the night, toward Thora's farm and beyond.

The yard at Otterness blazed with light. Light poured from open doors and from every window, cutting pale yellow squares into every dark wall.

The porch door stood open. As I walked through it, Johanna came from the house as though she'd been waiting there for me.

She pulled me into the living room. "I knew you'd come. Have you brought news?" Her eyes, red-rimmed and frantic, stared from her bloodless face and searched mine for hope, then turned away, disheartened, before I could shake my head in reply.

Nan stood off in the middle of the room, watching, silent and wooden, hugging her elbows against her middle, as if she were physically holding her splintered self together.

It was Johanna, churned again to life, who began to tell me what had happened. She spoke in short, agitated spurts, alternately clasping and waving her hands.

"He just disappeared. One minute he was here, then, just gone. The storm...we were all busy running about, so much to do. We'd had Andrew call Bea MacDonald to see if she needed help. Ross is gone, you see—"

"To Edinburgh!" Nan broke in inconsequentially. "Of all the times to go." As though he should have foreseen the storm. Perhaps, like me, she had suspicions about his absence.

"I'm so worried about her," Johanna whispered. Her distress had deepened, widened to include Nan. "She's been my stay, my comfort. But suddenly, with this helplessness . . . There's nothing we can do, you see, but wait. It's all made worse for her that Andrew has gone from her house, gone on the bicycle she and Uncle John gave him."

Johanna moaned softly, her own despair scarcely disguised, and rattled on. "But Bea told Andrew she needed nothing. So John went on his way to Thora's, to see about her sheep. Ours, too, we needed to inspect. Such a fierce gale, and with some hail as well, you see, which can injure them. But our sheep, they're hardy. Thora's, though, are pampered beasts. And we are still neighbors, you know, even though she's dead—" She stopped suddenly, her eyes wide, as though surprised at her own words, as though she, too, had been defending herself by refusing to remember Thora's death. For a moment her face crumbled, and I reached out for her, in case she might break down. Then she shook herself and resumed telling me her story.

"We stayed here, Nan and I—and Andrew, or so we thought." She turned to Nan for confirmation, or simply to keep gentle contact. Nan nodded numbly. "There are fences and gates perhaps needing attention, as well as animals, and John took Munro to Thora's . . ."

She closed her eyes and drew in her breath, squaring her shoulders. When she opened her eyes she looked at me unwavering, her voice decisive as she said, "Andrew's not in real danger, you know. He went off on his own somewhere for a reason. I don't know why. He wouldn't do such a thing, go off without telling us.

"But he did. He took his bicycle. We weren't aware just then, each of us assuming Andrew was with the other, until John returned. Then John took Munro out to find him. Munro did his best, though he wanted to search the fields and probably beyond to the cliffs, where he might normally look for lost sheep. That's what he's bred for, sheep. Border collies are meant to herd, to look and listen, not to track. At any rate, how could he track a bicycle on the tarmac? And in all this wet.

"But Andrew did go off on his own, he wasn't taken or—" Her resolve began to falter. "Why did he go like that?" she asked plaintively, her voice finally quavering. "I thought he was with Nana," she said, using Andrew's childlike form of address for her, "and Nana thought he was with me." Her confusion showed in her face. "He wouldn't just go off..."

I wondered if it would help them to know that Andrew, at least once before, had gone off exploring where he wasn't allowed to go alone. But it was true he wouldn't have done that now, at night, and certainly not on his bicycle. I decided to say nothing about last summer.

"...if he'd been struck by a car," Johanna was saying, her voice rising almost to a wail, "on the side of a road somewhere. Constable MacFee is getting men together. John has taken Munro and gone out along the road. If Andrew is near, Munro will find him. I wish—" She stopped. No need to articulate what she wished, and no use to do so.

It would be better for them to be busy doing something, even searching in unlikely places, than to agonize here.

"Do you want to go looking yourselves," I asked, "you and Nan? I'll stay, to be here when he comes home." I tried to coax a smile. "Shall I scold him when he returns, or leave that for you?"

Time seemed to stop as soon as they left, the wait already seeming interminable. I searched for diversion. I examined with care the collected bits of nature, the seashells, the hollow bird eggs, the round empty nest of a paper wasp, the still pungent curl of dried seaweed. But they only made me worry more about Andrew, their collector.

I thought of the day of Thora's death. Of her gold. Andrew might somehow have heard of Ben Gowan's find. Thora must have known of it, and could have told him. His meeting with her at the hermitage may have formed a bond between them closer than he'd admitted. They'd made a blood pact, after all. Andrew had accepted her, as children sometimes do odd people, without prejudice, unaware of their oddness. And Andrew was certainly closer in age to Thora than was Ivor Denison, or Thora's friend, Bea MacDonald.

Andrew was bored with hunting seashells. He wanted an important discovery. But even the promise of a *real* treasure, such as he'd searched for last summer, like the one he'd spoken of last night, found by a boy, could not have tempted him away from home in the dark, in the storm.

And an animal bone would have done as treasure for Andrew, or a pottery shard decorated by the thumbnail of an ancient hand, or a piece of worked flint. He didn't need gold.

I tried to remember my conversation with Thora in her studio. Had she said anything that would provide some clue? But I remembered none of her words, only her face close to mine, the swirling images of threads and colors, and the leering, golden eyes of the gripping beast brooch.

Why had Thora needed to be so secretive? If only she'd told me, or MacFee, how she acquired the gripping beast, maybe she wouldn't now be dead, maybe Andrew would now be home and safe. But she had been true to herself, evasive and enigmatic. And true, too, to her homeland, this mysterious, contradictory place.

Here, behind crashing surf and craggy cliffs, stretched out low hills and pastures, at once both wild and pastoral. Here flowers bloomed out of the bones of the violent past. Fence posts imitated gravestones. Hooves of sheep and cattle kicked up hidden silver and gold, or opened the craws of forgotten graves. Pillaging Vikings were transformed into Orkney farmers. A bloody Viking warrior became a saint.

Nothing was clear here, nothing straightforward.

... and nothing is but what is not, Macbeth had said, no more confused than I.

Even the name of this place was a paradox. The other islands—Stronsay, Westray, and the rest—had place names that, in Norse, described them as islands. Only this island was not named in that way, neither in Norse nor in Gaelic. Mainland, this, the largest island, was called.

Thora's weaving, so like the one she'd cut from her loom on the morning of her death, still sprawled over the piano in the living room. I approached the weaving, and took up a corner of it, looking at it more closely than I had the one on Thora's loom.

A summer-winter weave, Nan had called it. On one side a deep blue design on white, and on the other, the reverse. The white might be the winter snow, or the endless brightness of the summer sky. The blue might be the summer, or the cold winter blue of the sea. Or the deep darkness of tonight's midnight sky.

Both sides were different yet the same, winter and summer alike. Different yet the same, like the Orkney Islands themselves.

But that contradiction was part of what was happening.

I had dropped the corner of the weaving and turned from it. Now I turned back. My dream was not far away. Andrew's disappearance seemed more a shadowy continuation of it than reality. Thora had been in my dream, bending over her loom just as I'd seen her that morning of her death, with blood dripping from her face.

I searched the plain border of the weave for a mark. There, near the fringe, was a small brown spot. Was this what I was looking for?

Nan had said Thora made several summer-winter weavings. But I was convinced now this was not just one of many. Thora had cut this very weaving from the loom on the morning of her death. She'd ranted at me, waving her scissors, and drew blood from her own chin. She'd knotted and cut the warp. That drop of blood had marked her progress.

And at some time that morning after I had left and Thora had gone to her sickbed, at some time that morning before Thora had died, the weaving had found its way to Spindrift for Nan to buy.

Thora had not stayed at home with a headache, as Bea Mac-Donald had said. Thora had not stayed away from the Festival deliberately, as Ivor Denison had said.

Faces came to me then, and with them, words. Words that wove themselves through the Orkney paradoxes to form a warp and weft of meaning around what was happening. I heard in my mind the words Ross had spoken to me and Constable MacFee. I heard the words of Bea MacDonald. I heard Andrew. I heard John. I heard Thora herself, and I heard even my own words that morning in the police house.

I had believed Thora was killed so that someone could find the Viking treasure. But like the weaving, like the Islands, this, too, had a different side. All those words now told me what it was.

I lifted the telephone, but its silence rang back in my ear.

It was just as well, I thought. A woman, alone and unthreatening, might be better able to rescue Andrew than an army of men.

Those words told me where he was, and who had taken him there. I hoped I could get to him before he came to harm.

Twenty

That way the noise is.
—MACBETH, ACT V, SCENE vii

How long had Andrew already been gone? No one had said. How long had it been dark? I couldn't know how much time remained for me to reach him. I needed to hurry, but I didn't want to end up lost in the dark, and with Andrew still in danger.

I wrote a hasty note and left it beside the telephone telling my destination—my hoped-for destination. Once through the gates and pastures, I could follow the fowlers' path. But would I find the path? One pasture would look like another. I'd need light, along with plenty of luck. Johanna and Nan had taken flashlights from a kitchen drawer. Two remained, and I took one, clicking it on and off to be sure it worked. I took two batteries as well, and stuffed one into each of my jacket pockets.

From the jumble of outdoor gear beside the front door I grabbed the only walking stick remaining there. Andrew's shepherd's crook. I shouldn't need it to ward off the birds, but I might need it to keep my footing in the dark.

Yesterday Andrew had raced ahead of me and John to open the gates. I hadn't watched him, hadn't noticed their fastenings. The first gate I came to now was held fast by a rain-swollen wooden pin wedged tight in a hasp. My stiff, cold fingers refused to work it free. For several minutes I struggled, until the simple expediency of climbing over the gate occurred to me.

From here I could barely make out the second gate straight across the field, just on the edge of the light. I tried to run to it. The uneven ground, so easily negotiated yesterday even in my oversized boots, turned my run into a stumble. I slowed again to a walk.

The second gate opened freely, and the next, and I passed quickly through them, securing them behind me.

Where to now? We'd made one unmistakable turn in our wanderings yesterday from pasture to pasture, and I thought now I had reached that place. It seemed right, but still I turned uncertainly, and followed the new fence line with some apprehension.

The land dipped briefly, and became softer underfoot. On the other side of the fence the yellow irises Andrew had made a point of not picking yesterday emerged with pale luster from the night. I was going in the right direction. I proceeded more surely now, to another gate.

That, too, opened easily, but only darkness loomed beyond. I hadn't counted gates yesterday, or noted distance or direction, but I thought we'd crossed a large stretch of pasture soon after we saw the irises and right before we reached a final gate. But which way?

I stood for precious moments, taking myself back. I could remember only the grasses blowing, the sheep crowding back from us, the red Highland cattle grazing peacefully over the faraway hills. I shone my flashlight into the empty night, but its beam faded before touching substance. To strike out across the wide meadow would risk missing the gate, or going the wrong way. I would have to walk the perimeter of this fence the long way around, and hope that the first gate I reached was the right one, the only one.

I heard scuffling and occasional faint bleats around me, and made out the dim whitish mounds that were huddled sheep, sleeping through what remained of the night. I picked my careful way over the hummocky, close-cropped green. I had no idea how long it took. Forever, it seemed. The longer I walked, the slower I felt.

Over the nagging inner voice telling me I was lost, and too late besides, I assured myself that the land was ascending, that I was nearing the coast, that were it not for the animal noises and the rushing wind I would soon hear the boom of the storm-wracked sea, and smell its briny air. But the fence stretched on and on, unbroken.

Just as that inner voice convinced me I'd somehow ended up in the wrong pasture or simply missed the gate, I came upon an opening. And I remembered. The last fence had no ordinary gate, but a narrow gap, a staggered break in the fence that doubled back upon itself, like one turn of a labyrinth. Impossible for sheep and cattle, or even dogs, to negotiate. I remembered Munro scraping under the fence beside it, leaving a tuft of hair on the wire. And I remembered Andrew's blushing face, his ticklish smile, when he'd told me it was called a kissing gate.

I felt a grin spread across my face, but my sense of victory lasted only long enough to see me through to the other side. Now fences were behind me. Now I had to find the fowlers' path. And I had to find the right place to leave it.

Again I grinned. John's voice came to me, his enigmatic counsel, "You canna always see, so you must learn to listen."

Though he hadn't been talking about finding the fowlers' path, I thought I knew, I hoped I knew, what his admonition meant. It would benefit me later, but I could use it now as well. The path roughly paralleled the cliff edge, and ran between me and the sea.

If I walked toward the sounds, now unmistakably the surging and crashing of the waves, I would come upon it.

Out here the land had never been grazed. The wild grasses grew thick and tall, presenting new obstacles. The tangled stems of thistles and bedstraw caught at my legs. Wet blades and leaves slipped under my feet. Sharp stony inclines thrust up through the ground to trip me.

When I did fall, I fell on my stick with a heavy thud, my breath momentarily knocked out of me. I let go of the flashlight. It bounced and went out. I could see little now besides the black shadowy ground, the dark vegetation silhouetted against the barely brighter expanse of drifting, clouded sky. Still on my knees, I found the flashlight. I shook it, then rapped it against my thigh. Nothing happened. I sat back and felt the light cautiously with my fingertips. The lens had shattered and fallen out. One quick, sharp touch told me that the bulb, too, had broken. The flashlight was useless. I dropped it, and left it there.

Surprisingly, after a few blinded steps my eyes began to adjust. The darkness was not absolute. Shapes emerged in three dimensions. I could distinguish solid rock from clumps of grass, could avoid wading through dense thickets of weeds. My progress without the flashlight was scarcely slower than it had been with it.

The clouds were blowing away. The wind brought with it now an occasional fine mist, and I licked its salty wetness from my lips. Sea spray. Spindrift. No, Spindrift was the craft co-op in Digerness. Spindrift, where Andrew's peril had begun. I would soon be with him. At least I was finally near enough for the sea spray to wet my face.

I had expected to know the fowlers' path only when the springy growth beneath my feet became firm earth. Instead I saw it, a pale strip of ground lit by the reflection of the sky's dim light, by my father's *simmer dim*, in the pools of water in its ruts.

Until now I had worried more about finding my way than about Andrew. Now his image came before me, his face vulnerable and terrified. The urge to run to him, so close now, was almost irresistible. I spoke aloud to him as I climbed, adding my own quiet voice to the sounds of the night. "I know where you are. I'll save you."

The path was becoming harder to follow. Its borders, overgrown and ill defined at best, played lost-and-found. Its edges sometimes met, the path then disappearing all together. But somewhere, when the path had bypassed the weather-ravaged clifftops, it would be safe to leave it. When I reached that place I would know it, I was sure of that. John had told me.

I whispered, "I'm coming, Andrew."

Then I stepped into a hole. A hole dug by some scurrying hill creature, a rabbit or a stoat. And as I fell I heard a sound, a faint crack. I felt no pain. I was weary, I was frightened, I was cold, but I felt no pain. Yet I knew I had broken my ankle.

What would I do now? Tears flooded my eyes and sobs shook my shoulders. "God, why can't you help me?" I cried in an angry whisper. I wanted to scream it, to stand up and throw out my arms, to appeal not only to God but to Bea's St. Magnus, and to the pagan gods of the gripping beast. "He's only a child. Let me help him."

I got to my hands and knees, fighting the desire to curl up into a ball. With my weight still on my hands, I pulled my feet beneath me. Then, gingerly, I tried to stand. I couldn't. I fell again, and vomited into the long grass.

I wiped my mouth with a handful of grass, and then with the corner of my jacket. Something rolled from my pocket. The flashlight battery. What good could it do me now? What good could anything do me?

I struggled up again, this time pulling myself up with the help of the walking stick. I tucked the crook under my arm. Too long, it dug into my armpit, but when I hung on with both hands, it took my weight. I took one swinging step, and then another. The stick supported me.

There couldn't be far to go now. I listened to the sounds of the birds. They were fewer now than in daylight, and their individual cries more distinguishable. A large dark bird flew overhead and screamed as it passed. Another, smaller, keened on its way.

I hobbled on, step, stop, step, stop. A pain began, throbbing but bearable. I shivered, and gave in to it, to shivers that might warm me, might calm the spasms in my abdomen. I continued to pray, to beg. "Let him be all right. He's only a boy. Only a baby. Please, it's only a baby."

I was no longer sure for whom I was praying. Andrew's face swam before me, and my father's, and the crackled, bronzing photo-image of the face of an infant in my grandmother's arms, all strangely alike, all coming together as one. Almost unconsciously, I made a decision just then. My pregnancy, uncomfortable, inconvenient, unwanted, had become my unborn child. I could see its face. I made a kind of one-sided bargain. "I'll name him Andrew," I promised, "or Andrea. If only you'll keep us all safe."

I had to be near.

I heard a new bird call. I'd heard it before, but it had not come from the birds. It sounded exactly like Uncle John giving the call of the rare nesting petrels, the laughing cry of the Leach's petrels returning to their young, to their nooks and crannies amid the stones of the hermitage. Listen. That was what John had told me. This was the safe place to leave the fowlers' path.

A hot pain seared my leg now with every movement. I forced myself slowly on, following the petrels' calls, striving to keep them sorted from the low squeals and squabbles of the other birds. I knew Andrew was so near that if I said his name out loud he might hear me, that perhaps already he could hear the thudding of my heart.

Then I saw them, small dark birds with long forked tails, silhouetted against the sky in their darting, tentative flight. Midnight butterflies, ghost swallowtails, they were harbingers of deliverance. The hermitage was just ahead.

And Andrew. I saw him standing near the edge of the cliff, holding himself rigid, his arms straight down at his sides. He was turned from me. I couldn't see his face. I knew it would be white with fear, wide-eyed and bewildered. My heart pounded. For one horrible moment I thought I would be sick again.

I lurched closer. I saw it all now. On either side of me stretched out the long jagged sweep of the headland. In one direction its concave faces, now filled with sleeping birds, barely supported the great mats of sod that grew from the tops, balancing out into the air. I could see from here the stony maw of the empty tomb, the deeply undercut sides of the precipice beneath it. Not far off, in the other direction, balanced the bridged sea-stack that held the toppled remains of the tiny monk's cell. My body forgot to hurt. I forgot to retch. I forgot even to breathe.

Andrew stood before the grassy bridge that led to the hermitage. Between us, a few feet away from him, steadily pointing a gun at him, stood Bea MacDonald.

Twenty One

... the obscure bird
Clamored the livelong night. Some say, the earth
Was feverous and did shake.
—MACBETH, ACT II, SCENE iii

I hadn't expected she'd have a gun. I'd thought only as far as finding Andrew. After that, I'd simply planned to take him home.

And I had found him. Now what could I do?

The brief night was almost over. Openings in the clouds showed the faint glow of very early morning, growing quickly into true light. I was afraid I couldn't go on. I knew I couldn't reach Andrew without being seen by Bea. I was afraid I couldn't reach him without Bea shooting him.

Bea stood slightly to one side, her feet apart, planted solidly beneath her hips. She looked strong and secure. The tablets she took for her arthritic pain must have been potent indeed. She held the gun with both hands, close against her body, pointed at Andrew. Possibilities, questions, hopes, raced through my mind. Even without pain, would her bent fingers be able to pull the trigger? And surely if she did shoot, the recoil would knock her off her feet.

But might not that happen too late for Andrew?

Where had Bea got the gun? Was it Ben Gowan's, a souvenir of war? If so, it might be inoperable now after more than fifty years. But I couldn't count on that. Besides, an unpredictable weapon in the inexperienced hands of a woman on drugs might be the most dangerous situation of all.

A slight stir warned me that Bea had noticed me. She hadn't appeared to take her eyes from Andrew, hadn't moved until now, until that brief second when she turned just enough to bring me within the circle of her power.

"Bea!" The wind seemed to snatch the words from my mouth and whip them away behind me. I had to shout, and I had little strength for it. "Bea. Don't do this. He's just a boy. Bea. Let him go."

Andrew turned at the sound of my voice, his whole body moving together like an unarticulated china doll, solid and immobile. His round, white face shone like the moon.

"Don't worry, Andrew," I called to him untruthfully, trying to keep pain and despair from my voice, praying that he would believe me. "It's all over now."

And to Bea I shouted again, "Bea. Don't do this."

"I must." Bea spoke softly, yet from her lips the wind, blowing in from the sea, eerily carried every sound clearly to me.

"I need him," Bea went on. "The lad will make everything right again. He's the only one who can save us."

"Save us?" I said, almost to myself. "Save us from what?"

But I didn't need to ask. Save us from the reason we were here—Bea's confused, illogical beliefs, her religious fervor divided between God and ancient curses. "Hogboy? The Devil? Viking gods?"

Could Bea have heard me? Or perhaps, as earlier in my car, she didn't need to hear. "From the dead," she said. "We must give it back to the dead."

Bea must have been mad to have enticed Andrew to her, to have brought him at gunpoint to so treacherous a place, for this.

"Give what back, Bea?"

"The brooch."

"The gripping beast?"

For the first time Bea took her eyes from Andrew and turned to fully face me. "So you did know," she whispered. "Ross was right. You knew the whole time."

"No." I had to keep Bea's attention on talk, and not on my movements. I'd been moving closer, moving as much as I could, while I could. I wouldn't be able to move, or even stay standing, much longer. "I went to see Thora at her studio that morning. She wore the brooch. I saw it. But I didn't know, even then. I didn't suspect until yesterday it was part of the treasure your brother found."

I was close enough now to see Bea's face clearly, the whites of her eyes appearing as white circles around her dark, staring pupils, the lines at the corners of her tight, grim mouth confirming her implacability.

"Treasure!" Bea took the word and spat it back at me. "It was a treasure to no one. It killed my brother. He found a stone," Bea began telling me the story. "He was repairing the cottage wall. He thought that one stone was simply part of the wall at first, but a wee bit out of line, so he dug it out. Then he saw marks on it."

She didn't know my father had found the stone, and the marks, first. She didn't know her brother had recognized it.

"A few scratches only," she went on, "as most of it was worn smooth. He fussed and worried over it, and a few days later he announced it to be a rune stone. That's when he dug deeper, and found the rest. Grave-goods."

"It wasn't grave-goods, Bea."

"The same as. A memorial burial, he told me, belongings of

someone lost at sea or in a battle far away. But in a casket, and belonging to the dead. To take it was stealing from the dead. I warned him. 'Put it back,' I said. But he wouldn't listen. He suffered pains that very day."

"But he did put it back."

"Aye, he did, but too late. And he'd showed it to Ross. Ross wanted to sell everything on the sly. They quarreled. We both knew Ross would sell it if he could, would take Meggie and go away. That's why Ben agreed to bury the box again somewhere else, where Ross would never find it. But Ben told you where he put it. I saw the letters he wrote to you. No, come no nearer!"

I had tried to move closer. Bea had seen me move. It didn't matter. I couldn't walk anymore. I could only stand, hanging on with both hands to the stick, with the crook under my arm, hoping I could at least remain standing.

"I showed you the letters he wrote to me, Bea. He didn't tell me about the treasure."

But the truth didn't matter. Like Ross, Bea had her own truth. "What did you show me? There were other letters. If he didn't tell you, he told your father.

"Callum found that stone those many years ago. But no part of it belonged to Callum. No part of it belonged even to Ben. Nevertheless, Ben felt he owed a part to Callum. And so he told."

"He didn't." I cried now, from heartache and pain and sheer exhaustion. As I wiped my tears I turned to look at Andrew.

The petrels danced behind him in the air above the hermitage. Andrew stood near to where the waves broke, to where the highest, most storm-tossed of them sometimes washed completely over him. He stood drawn into himself, water dripping from him. He didn't seem to have moved at all. I silently willed for him to sink to the ground while Bea talked to me, to crawl through the grass, away from Bea's consciousness and her gun.

"Then you wrote him that Callum died. My brother died, too, but before he did I helped him rebury the chest and everything in it. Hamehollow was as much as he could manage. He'd already taken it there on his own, thrust it deep into a rabbit warren on the side of the hill. But right there was not safe, nor blessed, so we moved it above. A church stood there once, long ago, you see, and so still it was sacred ground. I thought, since we moved the grave goods, things would come right. And yet he died."

"So you tried to kill me."

"To scare you. To send you home. Thora gave you warnings, and she struck you once, but you were not deterred. You enticed my son, joined with him in the search. You went with him to the cottage, to where the chest had been found. Where would you lead him after that? I had to make you go. Your car sat in my yard. I called Thora. She made a wee slit in your brake line to cause a wee accident. You weren't even hurt."

"You couldn't be sure."

"I had to try. Nothing would have happened had you gone home. Or not come here in the first place. I couldn't let you lead Ross to the gold. If he finds it he will die. Or leave. Either way it will end the same. He'll be gone from me."

"And Thora? She helped you, and you killed her." Not in order to find the treasure, but to keep it hidden.

"The gold killed her. She couldn't resist that one piece. A shiny bauble. She had to have it."

"Why Thora? Why did she even know about it?"

"This place is hers." Bea swept out an arm to the hermitage, and noticed Andrew again. She moved back a step to keep us both in her sight. "She often went out there. Her magic place, she called it. But a holy site, too, you know. That's why I gave her the chest, told her to hide it. I told her its being there would make her powers stronger. I couldn't leave it at Hamehollow, not with you around, knowing its presence there, leading Ross."

"But I wouldn't lead Ross. I didn't know."

"Aye, so you say," sighed Bea. "So you say. But my brother wrote to you after we buried the chest, and here you came. And Thora said she felt danger..."

How much had Thora already known when we met? Had her theatrics on the pier been even then of Bea's design, or had they been genuine, the one true, if misguided, deed in this tragedy?

Bea answered my unvoiced question with a shake of her head. "Thora knew you were coming. We all knew. Ross learned from Meggie and he told me. He didn't know I'd helped Ben bury the gold. He thought I'd be happy for him to find it, for you to lead him to it."

"Thora said she felt danger." I repeated Bea's earlier words. I shuddered. The cold in my center had hardened into bitter ice. The pain in my ankle reeled through my brain now. My shoulder felt wrenched and torn, and both my arms trembled uncontrollably. But the shudder had been for Thora. For Thora and her portent of danger, which came true, but for herself instead of me.

"The danger came from you. I didn't kill her. Thora took the brooch," said Bea coldly. "You saw her. She pinned it to that plaid she wove, that wanton thing. She wore it that morning. We were the only two at the co-op so early. She announced she would keep it for herself. I warned her. I tried to make her understand. We had to put it with the rest. Keep everything together. Sacred.

"She agreed to do it." Her words were coming faster, her sentences hurtling together. "We went up to Hamehollow. I thought we could keep it there till nighttime, till she could bring it here. It would be back in hallowed ground. It would prove we were trying, wouldn't it? The brooch would be safe. We would be safe. But when we got there she wouldn't go through with it. She wouldn't put it in the ground. Too pretty, she said. Too pretty."

Her gift from the dead, Thora had told me, before I understood what she was saying.

Bea shook her head. "She wouldn't listen. I couldn't make her understand. She was running away from me, jumping to the top of the wall, running along it, singing her magic songs. I caught one of her legs. She came down then, quick enough. But she didn't stop. She laughed, jumped up again. I picked up a stone—"

Bea looked at me then with a shocked expression, as though it had just occurred to her, as though perhaps she had just read the thought in my mind, that the stone might have been a piece of the old church.

"I threw it," she said in a breathless, rising voice. "It hit her head, knocked her down. But it didn't kill her, not that stone. It was the gold, I tell you," she cried, pleading, then calmly again said, "I seized the brooch. Now Andrew must put it back in the chest with the rest, out on the stack."

I nodded, agreeing. "To save us. All of us. So don't let it kill Andrew, too."

Bea smiled, an eerie Cheshire grin in the morning light. "Don't worry, lass. He proved to me he could do it. He's a grand climber, don't you remember? Remember how he scaled the ladder at Spindrift, and took down the quilt for his Nana? Remember how he boasted of his prowess? Children have no fear of these things. I have a lad of my own, my Ross. I know."

She turned toward Andrew, and asked him, "You're not afraid, are you, lad?"

He looked at her with his blank moon face and didn't reply.

"No, Bea," I pleaded once again. "This is no ladder in a shop. The storm. The wind. It's wet. The grass is slippery. He'll fall. I fell myself, just coming here. Look." I tried to move closer, to show Bea my ankle, swollen now, and purple, and my wet shivering body, as though they might convince this mad, frightened woman. But I couldn't move. My head spun. I swayed. All that kept me upright was my good leg locked beneath me, my body propped on the walking stick, precariously tilting under me now, and perhaps, at last, God, in the mysterious way He'd chosen to help. If He had.

In my despair I recalled the dead whom Bea was trying so desperately to appease.

"Why not the tomb, Bea? Must everything be together? Surely the tomb is as sacred as the hermitage. More so. The tomb belongs to the dead, Bea. Let Andrew put the brooch in the tomb."

I saw Bea's eyes dart to the ancient tomb and back to Andrew. She walked slowly past him, turning as she crossed in front to keep the gun pointing at him. She held it, again, straight out, but her arms posed different angles than before, as though the dank chill had invaded her body also, and brought back her pain. She stepped stiffly, carefully, backward to the edge of the tomb. I held my breath as Bea peered over her shoulder into its invisible depths before lifting her head.

"No," Bea said. Her voice was tremulous, but she said it with finality. "Andrew will go out on the stack. I've given him the brooch. Now he'll put it back. He'll crawl if he must. He'll place the brooch in the chest with the rest, and he'll crawl back."

Even from this distance I could see that Bea's jaw was set, her posture rigid. She wouldn't waver.

Again I swayed. My hands slipped on the stick. I would collapse soon. Bea would become impatient with talk. Our time had almost run out, mine and Andrew's. I had to do something. And now.

"I have to sit, Bea," I said. I half sank to the ground, and half fell, trying as I did to fall closer to her. The world around me went black for an instant. I couldn't faint now. I summoned what strength remained.

I hadn't come close enough to Bea. The shepherd's crook would not reach her. I let go of it, and shoved one hand into my pocket. My fingers closed on the remaining flashlight battery, the one I hadn't already lost in my trek here. It was no match for a desperate woman with a gun, but now especially, with Bea weakening and in pain, it might startle her, provide a diversion. However feeble, it seemed our only hope.

I flung the battery at Bea's face. As if in slow motion, I saw Bea turn and point the gun directly at me. I saw her cock it. I saw her trigger finger tense and pull. I heard the gun go off.

I'd read that when you're shot at you don't hear the gun, or the bullet whistling toward you. But I heard the shot. It made an appalling sound that filled my head, that made me want to cover my ears, to shout at Bea to stop making so much noise. I wasn't hit, of course. That was why I heard the gun. Bea had missed.

But she hadn't. I felt warmth in the bend of my arm. I felt a constricting pain, like someone had tied a tourniquet around my upper arm and was twisting it too tight. Bea hadn't missed after all. But I wasn't dead. There was still a chance for Andrew.

I opened my mouth to call to him, to tell him to run. But another sound, louder, more terrible than the sound of the gun, thundered through the night. As it roared and reverberated down to the sea and back, Andrew ran to my side and dropped onto the grass beside me.

The ground trembled beneath us. The morning light dimmed behind a great cloud of dust. The noise rumbled on, its echoes rolling across the clifftop in a ceaseless barrage.

I lifted my head. The tomb and the place where Bea had been standing were gone.

Birds filled the air. Auks, guillemots, fulmars, and kittiwakes, their slate nests wrenched out from under them, flew in confused circles, screaming for their young.

Andrew and I crouched together, our arms tight around each other, until at last the roar of the avalanche stopped. The sounds of the birds still crying, and the scree still skittering down the cliff face, settled over us like a blessed silence.

Twenty-Two

...for the poor wren,
The most diminutive of birds, will fight,
Her young ones in her nest, against the owl.
All is the fear and nothing is the love.
— MACBETH, ACT IV, SCENE ii

T wo days later I found Ross.

Andrew and I had been rescued by a vindicated Munro, who had come home with John at daybreak—and, like John, exhausted, unsuccessful, and heartbroken—finally to be allowed to search where he'd known all along we would be. He'd led MacFee and Uncle John and a party of men to us, a party that had marched up noiselessly, toting blankets and stretchers and first-aid supplies.

They carried us down to waiting warmth and light, to Johanna and Nan and Graham Sinclair.

I remembered little else of the remainder of that night, of that dreamlike early morning. I woke in Balfour Hospital in Kirkwall later that day, after having endured the setting of my ankle and the removal of the bullet from my arm, and luxuriated in hours of deep, healing sleep.

Johanna visited first, bringing me a sheaf of tissue-wrapped flowers.

"These are from all of us. They come from the florist. I wish they were field flowers, like those Andrew...I wish...how can we thank you? You saved Andrew's life."

Though Andrew and I had talked to our rescuers, we'd each babbled our own weary, incoherent, incomplete tale. Johanna knew only the little that Andrew had told her, the little that Andrew himself knew. She knew only that Bea MacDonald had tricked him away to perform a mad, treacherous task.

"Bea first spoke to him at Spindrift, on Festival day," Johanna told me. Her words tumbled out in a sudden cathartic rush, as though telling me the parts I didn't know would ease their distress, hers and Andrew's. "She told him she would need his help soon, and that he mustn't tell me or anyone. He thought it must involve a surprise for me or Nan. When the storm came she would have known we'd call to see if she needed us—and with all there was to do, with Andrew always wanting to be involved in some way, she must have guessed that in our hurry we'd have him do our telephoning for us. Or it was luck. She had plenty of that. Luck for her that no one saw him. Luck he didn't tell. He's a thoughtful child. And obedient. He thought he was doing something fine, obeying an elder, and helping his neighbor 'without trumpets,' as the Bible tells us to do.

"He went to her on his bicycle to Pentwater, as she asked. She had him hide it in a shed, to be safe from thieves, who were about, she said. He actually held her, half carried her on the walk up to the cliffs. It was only when they were there, near the precipice, that he began to worry. The hermitage frightened him. Something to do with Thora."

I nodded, ready to tell her, but she didn't notice. She didn't wait for me to explain. Did it matter any longer?

"He wanted to go home. That's when she took out the gun. Her brother's, I suspect. From the war. Why else would Ben Gowan have a gun? In Orkney we don't need guns." Tears filled her eyes.

"She might have killed him. Or you. We're so grateful, Isabel."

"No, you shouldn't be. It all happened because of me. Bea needed Andrew to hide the treasure from me."

Johanna's eyes widened, her tears washing over unheeded, and she shook her head in disbelief.

"She thought I could find its hiding place," I went on. "She was afraid I'd lead Ross to it. She had to move it to a new place, a new safe, sacred place. And she had to have help to do it. First Thora—"

"I still can't believe Bea killed Thora," Johanna cried. "Oh, I know she did, she confessed to you she did. And she tried to kill Andrew. But she isn't evil, nor greedy. So why?"

"If it hadn't been for me, if I hadn't come here, she wouldn't have. She wouldn't have believed she had to. It was fear that drove her, not greed or evil, but fear of losing Ross. Without me, none of this would have happened."

"Or if you'd taken Thora's warning and gone home?" Through her tears Johanna laughed at me, her face coloring almost to normal. "Nonsense! Don't blame yourself. Like Andrew—" She paled again, and she dropped into the chair beside my bed.

"How is he?" I asked.

"Such a wee lad, to be subjected to such happenings! He's quite distressed. His father has come. We'll take Andrew home to Inverness, and perhaps even to Edinburgh to a special children's doctor there. And then I hope we'll bring him back here. I don't want him to remember Digerness as a sad and frightening place. I want him to know it as happy and safe, and full of love."

After Johanna, Graham visited, but offering a book as well as hothouse flowers. He hesitated before he handed the book to me. "Perhaps you'd rather not have this, after what happened to you," he said.

He must have bought it for me before the ordeal on the cliffs. It was about the wildlife of Scotland, with a photograph on its cover of a Leach's petrel hovering over a heap of lichen-crusted stones. Pain stabbed through me at the sight of it, and for a moment old fears came back. I decided he was probably right, but I managed to say, "Not for today, but someday—I will enjoy it. Thank you."

He sat, his hands clasped in front of his knees, his head lowered. "I suppose you'll be leaving Orkney soon, going home."

"Not for maybe a month, the doctor says."

The bullet wound had been minor, even now healing well. My ankle had suffered an incomplete break, but I wouldn't be using it much, even with a walking-cast, for a while. And the doctor wanted me to stay in Orkney for a time to rest, more for my baby's sake than because of my broken bone. I'd agreed. Besides, I wanted to stay. I didn't want to remember Digerness as a sad and frightening place, either.

"But after that, yes, I suppose I will."

"Will you be returning?" When I didn't answer immediately, he peered up at me, his head still bowed. "I'd like for you to come back."

"If I did, I wouldn't be alone." I took a deep breath. "I'm having a baby, you see. I was going to be married, but now I'm not. And I wasn't going to . . ." But I wouldn't discuss with Graham, with anyone, the action I'd considered. Especially now, since in my fear for Andrew I'd decided almost without conscious thought to keep my baby, and the decision, once made, now seemed inviolable. "I'm having the child," I told Graham, "and raising it myself."

I thought he might recoil from me, might even leave. Instead, he said, with an uncertain, hopeful grin, "Digerness would be a grand place to raise a child."

But I had one more confession to make. "For a while I wondered if you'd killed Thora. I was afraid you had."

Unexpectedly, he laughed. "Is that why you pushed me away? I thought . . . what a relief! I can't imagine, though, why you should have considered that."

"You knew about Ben Gowan's find. But you weren't present when Ross told Constable MacFee and me about it. You even knew the treasure was probably from a memorial burial."

"Ben had discussed it with me. Hypothetically. He never declared what he had for certain, and of course I never saw any of it, but from his descriptions, I surmised that much. And from that you assumed I was guilty?"

"You knew more than you should. And you showed me the gripping beast design. I wondered why you did. It was when I saw it that I realized Thora could have been wearing one of the pieces from the Viking hoard before she died. I thought you might be trying to see my reaction, to gauge how much I knew, or guessed."

Graham nodded, accepting my unclear reasoning. "Pure coincidence. I never realized Thora's involvement, nor your involvement with her. Nor even, beyond your finding her body, that you knew her.

"I'm sure Ben had ethical concerns about his discovery, and his hiding of it, but his family worried him even more. I doubt he suspected just how serious the situation with his sister really was. Poor Thora. What a shame he didn't announce his find.

"Or perhaps the fault was mine. Perhaps I should have broken his trust, and told someone. If either one of us had, we'd have prevented all this. Ben would have gained fame in his final days. And beyond. He'd discovered a memorial stone as well, I understand. The name-stone served the dead for remembrance. It would have done the same for Ben."

My father had found it first, but that no longer mattered. "Bea knew he'd found the name-stone," I said, "but she never said she valued it. Could it still be there, in the cottage garden?"

"Aye, perhaps it could. Poor Bea as well. She tried to save souls and appease gods. But she concerned herself about the wrong objects. The burial goods had import, surely, but spiritually the stone was the important part, most often the only part of a cenotaph. The stone that declared the name of the dead."

Graham came for me at the hospital the next morning to take me to Furrowend. Nan had offered to care for me at the farm, but she had worries enough. As long as Meggie would have me, I would try to manage on my own at the inn. Meggie would help. The inn and the restaurant were otherwise closed for a few weeks at least, while her parents retreated together to Tenerife.

On the way to the inn I asked Graham, "Has Meggie heard from Ross?"

"No. Nor has he been turned up yet in Edinburgh. And Air and Sea Rescue has found no sign of Bea."

Ross had honestly loved his mother. I'd seen it in his teasing face when he was with her. He would be devastated when he finally arrived home from his unaccountable trip and learned of her fate. I wouldn't intrude on his grief to talk to him then about the cottage. But it had occurred to me I might want to live there in the summer, or possibly even year-round. I'd wondered if one day Ross might sell it to me.

I asked Graham, "Do you suppose it would be all right if I visited his cottage?"

Graham considered, and nodded.

"Would you take me there now?" I wanted to see it again. But more than that, I needed to sit again for a little while in my father's upstairs room. "You could leave me and then come back."

"I'll wait for you," he said. "I'll help you."

He wanted to carry me up to the cottage. He settled for lifting me from the car, and walking beside me while I struggled with my crutches, holding me when I wavered. After that, he leaned over, lifted my chin and kissed me, and for once I responded. I was not yet ready for passion, but its beginnings stirred between us, and more than that, affection. His kind arms encircling me, the core of strength beneath his comforting chest, tempted me to cling. Here in the sunshine, with no turmoil or suspicions to distract me, I noticed the dimples that creased his cheeks when he smiled, the lines that habitual laughter had engraved on his face, and the amber lights that sparked in the brown of his eyes.

I thumped along beside him, up to the cottage, where I would sit on the first hall step and work myself up to my father's room one at a time. The untamed blue flowers that had bloomed over the garden path were, after these few days, all overblown. A way had been trampled through the overgrowth to the front door.

As I opened the door I heard several bumps, and then a muffled growl, coming from the under-stair cupboard. A stack of propped lumber must have slipped and wedged against the door. Someone was trapped.

I shouted for Graham.

He lifted and dragged the wood away with no help from me, and as he pried the last board free, the cupboard door burst open. Ross crept out, bristled and dirty and reeking, his hands scraped and bleeding. Frayed duct tape flapped from his wrists.

Ross sat on the floor, his head resting against the wall. I sat beside him, on the first stair, and gave him small sips of water from a cup Graham had found in the kitchen sink, while Graham drove to the nearest telephone to call for an ambulance and for Constable MacFee.

Ross tried to talk while we waited. "My mother?" he rasped.

He didn't need to learn what happened just yet. "That's over now," I simply said, and he accepted that. Either he'd suspected, or his exhausted mind was not yet ready to have that question answered.

"Where's Thora? Mam was planning..." His speech was thick and slow. "Something odd. I tried to find out, maybe stop her, but... I think...

"After the Festival she brought me supper here. Something in my soup. Ben's old medicine? Woke up in there." His eyes flicked toward the cupboard. "Dark. Thirsty. Brutal headache. Wrists taped together." He lifted his wrists, a wry twist on his mouth. "Bloody tough stuff, duct tape."

"But she couldn't drive. How did she get around to do all this? With Thora, too—" I stopped myself in time. I hadn't intended to question him, or to tell him more than he should know right now.

"Mam not drive?" He tried to smile, and his hand shot up to his dry, cracked lips. "A farm woman? Doesn't much, but of course she can. Taught me."

He continued to talk. "She came back. Don't know when. I was pretty groggy. Fed me more soup, but I think that, too, was drugged..."

Her own son. Everything she'd done, she'd done to protect him, to keep him. I believed she'd have returned to free him. She'd almost killed him, but when she'd finished what her primitive fears had told her she must do, she'd have returned.

As the ambulance men wheeled Ross away he said, "The treasure?"

The Heritage Society would rescue the treasure. It probably would go on exhibit in Edinburgh and London, where crowds would line up to see it, and schoolchildren would study it and go back to their classrooms with its images in their heads to write essays about.

It couldn't remain where it now lay, on a wind-blown pinnacle above the sea. The site may have kept the Vikings from ravaging an indigent monk, but it would not keep treasure hunters from finding the gold. They would cross the bridge, or climb the stack from a boat anchored at its base.

A team from the university would soon begin taking the cottage garden wall apart, stone by stone, in search of the weathered name-stone. That, at least, might stay where it belonged, or a new stone would be carved for that place if the old, weathered stone could be deciphered. It would proclaim to the gods once again the name of the one whose death so long ago had begun these tragic events.

Only the gripping beast would never be studied, or admired, or wondered at.

On that awful morning, after the roaring had stopped, after the screeching and skittering had stopped, I had studied Andrew's face, so close beside mine. It seemed frozen in fear, pinched and drained, his eyes protuberant, black irises ringed with white.

"Here," he said, and I looked down at the hand he held out. His fingers uncurled. There in his palm lay the round, golden brooch.

" 'Tis hers, isn't it?"

He could not yet have assimilated the night's happenings. He had not yet surrendered the appalling responsibility Bea had given him for the brooch.

He said, in a tight, chattering voice, "I can pitch, too."

"What?"

"I can climb, but I can pitch, too."

My mind was hazy with pain and horror. From the steady,

muttering jangle of the birds still searching for their homes, an occasional scream would explode, and I would start. Every muscle in my body would strain to flee, and at the same time to hold and protect, to cling together with Andrew on the damp, solid ground. My whole awareness was a physical one. I couldn't comprehend what he was saying.

"Shall I?" he said. " 'Tis hers."

Finally I understood. I nodded.

Together we struggled upright. He held me to support me, and I held him to comfort both of us. Holding each other, we stepped once, twice, as far as I could, as close as we dared, to the shattered brink. Andrew drew back his arm and threw, and I watched the gripping beast arc and turn, the rising sun glittering off its staring eyes and its grasping hands and feet. I watched it drop, to join Bea MacDonald in the sea.

SANILAC DISTRICT LIBRARY